JENIFER STOCKDALE is an optioned screenwriter and novelist whose work explores the unsettling space where memory, truth, and family collide.

Her novel, Trigger, draws on her signature style - psychological thrillers where nothing is ever quite what it seems.

She is represented by One Moorer Management, has written and produced short films, and her scripts span thrillers, romantic comedies, and holiday features.

Trigger marks her first published book with Dark Anthem Press.

TRIGGER

A gripping psychological drama about fractured memory, family, secrets and the dangerous lies we tell to survive.

JENIFER STOCKDALE

This book is dedicated to all who have carried lies in place of memory – truth will prevail and light your way home.

Trigger Warning

This book contains references to suicide, childhood trauma, emotional abuse, and disturbing family dynamics.

Though the characters and events are fictionalized, the emotional truth behind them is real - shaped in part by the author's personal experience with the loss of a sibling to suicide.

Some stories insist on being told, even when no one wants to hear them. That said, trauma doesn't always respect coincidence. Sometimes, the trigger is real. The story is not.

Please take care while reading.

trig·ger /ˈtrigər/
noun : trigger ; plural noun : triggers

noun: a small tongue on a firearm that when pressed by the finger, actuates the mechanism that discharges the weapon. As in: "When Dora Cullen was eight, her favorite brother Tommy held a gun to his temple and pulled the trigger."

verb: trigger; 3rd person present: triggers; past tense: triggered; past participle: triggered; gerund or present participle: triggering

verb: to initiate or precipitate (a chain of events, scientific reaction, etc.). As in: "At fourteen-years old, Dora hears a song on the radio that triggers a series of memories which lead her to realize her brother's death may not have been what it appeared to be."

verb: (especially of something read, seen, or heard) to distress (someone), typically as a result of arousing feelings or memories associated with a particular traumatic experience.

Computing Definition: An action causing the automatic invocation of a procedure, for instance to preserve referential integrity when a user attempts to modify data with an insert, delete, or update command.

As in: "If Dora reveals her memories, a trigger will not allow her family, her friends, or her community to believe that her brothers are the sociopaths Dora knows they are."
At that point, Dora might as well use a trigger on herself.

Chapter 1

I am an Islander, or a native, or a Vineyarder. Any one of these words can be used to describe me. I think. Even though there are tons of names to describe people on the Island, I don't know of any that are used for people who were born there and then were forced to leave. There are names for people who came in the morning and left by evening: day-trippers, tourists, or cidiots. People who came for the summer were called "summer dinks" or "summer ginks", and then this could further be broken into the categories of July and August people.

We had the Yacht People, and we had names for the people who weren't born on the Island but moved there, which were wash-a-shores or transplants. As for Islanders who moved away, "traitor" might work, especially if the person moved to Nantucket. Or maybe "deserter," if they left because they wanted to, but for me, neither of those worked.

I never wanted to leave in the first place, and every single day I tried to get back. They kidnapped me, forced me to leave, locked me up and didn't let me go back. I just wanted to go home.

People here are always asking me what it was like to grow up on the Island, I didn't have an answer for them because I didn't know what it was like to not grow up there. I didn't think there was anything odd about the fact that pretty much everyone I knew was a drunk.

In the summer there were parties, the bars opened and stayed open late. In the winter, everything shut down, so the liquor stores stayed open late, and everyone sat at home and drank. To me, it was normal, it wasn't until I was older that I learned people from off-Island weren't like that.

I guessed my brothers and I were pretty lucky though, because our parents weren't alcoholics. Now that I was fourteen I was starting to see just how unique my childhood was. People always told me how lucky I was that I could go to the beach every day. I did do that, but the problem was we went to places like The Lagoon or Seth's Pool, actually, it was Seth's Pond, but that's what we called it. It was a freshwater pond in West Tisbury and it was kind of gross compared to the ocean.

We never went to the nice beaches like South Beach or The Bend in the Road because Mom didn't want to have to deal with the tourists and the impossible parking their presence created. Then winter would come, the off-Island people would leave, and there would be nothing to do. We barely got snow and most years the ponds didn't freeze enough to skate on.

Islanders were pretty particular about the things that tourists said. If somebody asked for directions to "Oaks Bluff" (instead of Oak Bluffs) it was customary to send them down a road that ended at the water, preferably one with enough beach sand to get them stuck.

When talking about where one is, "in Oak Bluffs" or "in Edgartown" is correct. Anyone saying "I'm in Martha's Vineyard" was obviously a first class idiot, people were on Martha's Vineyard not in it.

I only knew three people who were in Martha's Vineyard and they were all buried at the Oak Grove Cemetery, my Gram and Grampa and my brother Tommy. Gram and Grampa died from the standard ailments that afflict the elderly: a stroke and a heart attack, respectively.

My brother's official cause of death was suicide, but my Gram, until the day she died, swore my brother would never have done a thing like that and was convinced he was murdered. And what my mother always said about my

7

grandmother is that it wasn't actually a stroke that killed her, but it was her ideas.

When she got the one in her head about my brother and what he would or wouldn't do, it grew so big it couldn't be contained, and it just exploded. Those same ideas were the ones that have stopped me from being able to go home. Locked up, locked down, throw away the key. Dora is too crazy to even be around the drunken idiots.

People thought I knew a bunch of famous people. That wasn't true, well, not entirely. We saw famous people all the time, in line at the grocery store or getting their mail at the post office. The thing was, we didn't act all star stuck and try to get their autographs or anything. To us, they were just another group of tourists, another parking space taken up in the A&P parking lot.

So, I guess for me, growing up on the Island was no different than growing up anywhere else. I had two parents and four older brothers. We lived on a road that nobody but my parents drove down. Both of my parents worked at the hospital. My father was an orthopedic surgeon and my mother ran a satellite clinic for a shrink from the loony bin in Taunton.

When I was a kid I was totally spoiled and I was always the center of attention. Whenever I walked into the room whatever my parents or my brothers were talking about, they would stop and would talk to me, about whatever I wanted to talk about. The only problems I had with my childhood were my birthday and my name. Since my birthday marked the end of summer and the beginning of school, I got school supplies and Martha's Vineyard sweatshirts that were bought on clearance.

As for my name, I always wondered what kind of reefer my parents were smoking when I was born. Lucky for me, my grandmother wasn't in on their little smoke-fest and came up with my nickname, Dora. That was fine with me because that was less of a problem than my actual name, which was Adorable.

My brothers were obviously named when my parents weren't fucked up on some psychedelic shit. Jim was twelve when I was born, Tommy was ten, Pat was seven, and Donny was five.

I always assumed that I had a really shitty memory, because I couldn't remember a lot from my childhood. Even though I was eight, and not really that young when he died, I didn't remember my brother Tommy that well. No matter how hard I tried, I could only recall a couple of specific things about him:

When I started kindergarten, I had a hard time learning the difference between nickels and dimes. I didn't understand how a nickel could be bigger in size, but worth less than a dime. One day my brothers were hanging around the TV room watching a football game, when I found a coin in the bathroom.

I said to them, "I found a nickel on the floor. Did anyone lose one?"

"It's mine," Jim said. "I lost a nickel."

"You should never let anyone know how much you found," Tommy told me. "That way for someone to claim it, they have to tell you how much they lost."

"Hmm," I said, looking down at the coin in my hand and realizing it was a dime, not a nickel. "Thanks, Tommy. And Jim, I hope you find your nickel, 'cause I just found me a dime."

I left the room as they laughed at Jim.

Another time I had a loose tooth. It was hardly even loose but I wanted the tooth fairy to come, so I had to get it out. Even though Tommy was doing his homework, he stopped to help me. He tried tying a string to it and slamming the

9

door, but the string kept slipping off my tooth. After trying like twenty times, he told me he had to get his homework done, and I should just wiggle it until it came out.

I went into my room and took off my school clothes. I stood in front of my full-length mirror in my white t-shirt and underwear, wiggling it as hard as I could stand.

After about two hours, the front of my t-shirt was covered with blood and the tooth was only holding on by the very front part of my gum. But it was really stuck, so I could pull it down and it stayed in place, smushing my lip. I ran out of my room and down the hall to Tommy's. As I turned the corner I heard my mother call my name, but I kept going.

I yelled, "Tommy! Look!" but it came out, "Towy! Wook!" because of my smushed lip.

Before he could even answer, my mother was behind me grabbing my arm and yanking me out of his room and into the bathroom. While she checked my tooth and cleaned up the blood, she told me I had to be careful about the way I dressed in front of my brothers. I couldn't walk around in my underwear.

I would have to start thinking about how someday I was going to be a young lady and I would have to think about how I looked to other people. I didn't really understand why she thought my brothers would look at me in any strange way. They were my brothers. They wouldn't look at me any different if I was in my underwear than if I was fully dressed. I always walked around in my underwear. Nobody ever said anything about it before.

The next day there was a box on my bed waiting for me when I came home from school. In it was a bathrobe. The day after that my mother made a new rule that I wasn't not allowed to go into my brothers' bedrooms at all, and she made me switch rooms. I had to move into the baby room across the hall from her and dad's room.

I wasn't upset about it, even though my brothers thought I should have been and kept asking me if I was mad. The baby room was half the size of the room I had, which meant I couldn't even bring my furniture. My mother had just re-done the big room for me and bought me a beautiful canopy bed, a vanity table, matching dressers and nightstands. She wallpapered the room with really pretty flowered paper, and the new rug was so thick, I lost my feet every time I stepped on it. In the baby room, I could only fit a bed, without the canopy, and one dresser.

The walls were painted an icky yellow color, and only one tiny window looked out at the side of the garage. The bare floors were cold and hard, but I was happy to move in there. I would be safe across the hall from my mother. Nobody would dare come into my room in the night with my mother right there.

I woke up one morning and everybody in my house was in a panic, but nobody would tell me why. My mother was in my father's office making phone calls. Jim, Pat, and Donny were running around the house, looking in all the closets, cabinets, and drawers for something. My father was outside talking to a policeman.

My cries of, "Where's Tommy?" never got answered even as Donny and I were sent to walk our separate paths to school.

I got in trouble at school a bunch of times. I know I must have been a real problem for my teachers, I just couldn't sit still. The scene in my house that morning had just been too weird.

Sometime after lunch I got called down to the office. My teachers had already sent me there a few times because I got in trouble, but I didn't get called there. I was wicked nervous walking down the hall. When I rounded the corner where the office was, I saw Jim standing near the secretary's desk.

I prayed the reason why he was there had nothing to do with Tommy and that my mother forgot a dentist appointment or something. Then I figured if that's all it was, she would have come, not sent Jim, who should have been in school himself.

When I pushed open the office door, the first thing I noticed was how quiet it was. Everyone turned and looked at me. Then I saw that my brother had tears in his eyes. I knew then that something was terribly wrong and it had to do with whatever was going on at my house that morning. The secretary gave me a dismissal pass and Jim and I walked to the car without saying a word.

Donny was sitting in the back seat of the car. I slid in next to him and keeping his eyes straight ahead he said to me, "We ain't gonna see our brother Tommy no more. And that's it. You don't need to ask no questions."

Chapter 2

1982

I always felt bad that I wouldn't have many memories to share in case my family ever decided to sit around and reminisce about my brother. But lucky for me they didn't. It was like when he died, he had never even existed. Nobody mentioned his name again.

I guessed that since I was starting my freshman year of high school and my brothers were all either in college or had already graduated, my parents decided it was the right time to give up on their marriage.

They had not gotten along very well since my brother died. Sometimes they would go days, or even weeks without talking to each other.

I remembered being a little kid and sitting in the same room with my parents and my father would say, "Dora, tell your mother (whatever he wanted to say to my mother)" and my mother would say, "Well, Dora, you can just tell your father (whatever she wanted to say back to him)." And back and forth.

Of course, I never repeated what they said, because they were right there to hear each other, but they would still start each sentence with "Dora, tell your mother..." or "Dora, tell your father...."

Mom and I moved into a winter rental on the weekend after Labor Day and Dad stayed at the house. My parents were going to put our house up for sale the next spring, because the real estate agent told them nothing sold during the winter anyway. The arrangement wasn't so bad. I got to go see my Dad and my brothers on the weekend.

Shortly after we moved out, my mother started going to a single parents' support group. They convinced her that all children my age had a hard time with divorce and that she had to pay special attention to me. The truth was, it didn't really bother me all that much. My parents fighting had been more upsetting to me than their actual divorce was. Nobody yelled in our house and Mom seemed much happier.

Not that I would have told her any of that. She thought she should feel guilty for divorcing Dad and therefore spoil me. Her version of spoiling was to let me do whatever I wanted. I didn't ask her if I could do things anymore, I told her.

One Saturday Stacy called me and told me she was having a sleepover party, emphasis on party. She told me that she also had a surprise for me and that I should be ready. With Stacy, a surprise could mean pretty much anything.

So, ready meant I told my mother I was sleeping at Stacy's and that her phone was broken, so she could try calling but probably wouldn't get through. My mother didn't like Stacy, didn't think she was a good influence on me, but because of her idiotic support group, she let me go. This was pretty much the first time I regretted my mother not acting like a mother. But it wouldn't be the last.

When I got to Stacy's Brandy and Laurie were already there, but nobody else was, so it wasn't a big party, which is what I was thinking. And besides, Stacy's mother was home. Granted she was totally fucked up and in her bedroom, but I couldn't imagine the house was about to be run over by a hundred of our classmates carrying in kegs and bottles of booze.

Stacy led us down to her finished basement and had us all sit. She stood in the middle of the room with a huge smile and reached into her pocket, pulling out a baggy and holding it up to show us. There were three little pieces of paper with tiny strawberries on them.

"What is it?" asked Laurie.

"Stickers?" opined Brandy.

"Tattoos? Aren't we a little old to be doing that? " Laurie looked over at Brandy and they cracked up.

"Are you fucking serious right now?' Stacy complained. "I went through a lot of trouble to get this LSD and you think we're having a fuckin' kiddie tattoo party?"

"Well, I don't know what LSD looks like. I never seen it before. Are you serious? Those are for real?"

"Like honest to God, real LSD?" asked Laurie.

"You, my friends are about to go on a trip and you don't need to get a fucking boat reservation," Stacy said.

"Shit yeah."

"I've been wanting to do LSD forever."

I hadn't said a word, so everyone turned and looked at me. "I don't know, guys."

"Are you fucking kidding me, Dora? Are you a pussy or what?"

"It's not that."

"What is it then?" Stacy demanded.

"It's just I take this medicine -"

"Oh, here we go-"

"And I don't know if it'll have a reaction or whatever with it."

"What kind of medicine?" asked Laurie.

"Yeah, we never heard you talk about medicine," Brandy said.

"She doesn't take no medicine. She's a fucking pussy and is trying to get out of it without looking like one." Stacy said.

"I swear, look." I took off my shoe and spread my toes so they could see the needle pricks in between them.

"Dora, what the fuck is that?"

"It's from my shots." I spread my other toes where there were similar pricks.

"What kind of medicine goes between your toes?" Laurie asked.

"The kind you don't want anyone to know about." Stacy said. "Junkies do that all the time. Inject there so they don't get track marks. What the fuck, Dora? Are you a junkie?"

"Oh, yeah, my brother does that sometimes," Brandy shared.

"Seriously, Dora what the fuck is that shit?" Laurie asked.

"It's nothing. Forget it." I quickly put my shoe back on.

"Oh no. This is one genie that cannot be put back in the bottle. Why do you have needle marks between your toes?" Stacy asked.

"My mother says it's just so -"

"Your mother does that? What the fuck, Dora? This is so not normal."

"It's just for my nerves and she does it there so I don't have bruises, and then I don't have something else to be nervous about." I explained.

"That's bullshit. You're the least nervous person I know," Stacy said.

"Yeah, 'cause of the medicine," I said.

Stacy threw up her hands, "Whatever, Dora. Do what you want to. We're gonna do this and I could care less if you. There's something very wrong going on there, so maybe you should just go home, ask your mother what the fuck she's giving you. You ready, Brandy and Laurie?"

"Shit, yeah," Brandy jumped to her feet.

"Let's go sneak some beer to drink after," Stacy suggested. "I heard the acid tastes pretty bitter."

"I'll wait here. Bring me one." Laurie stretched out on the couch into the spot Brandy just vacated.

Stacy and Brandy headed for the stairs, but then Stacy turned back to me, as I hadn't moved. "Well, Dora? Did you forget where the exit is?"

"No, I'll stay. I mean, I'll do it."

"That a girl."

"This is going to be so fucking cool," Brandy followed Stacy up the stairs.

When they were out of earshot, Laurie spoke, making me jump out of my skin, because she had closed her eyes and I didn't expect her to say anything. "You don't gotta do it if you don't want to, you know. Don't let Stacy peer pressure you."

"She's not peer pressuring me. I wanna do it."

"Okay, as long as you're sure."

"I'm sure."

"What about your medicine?"

"It will be fine," I said.

"You know it is weird that she puts it between your toes," Laurie said.

I shrugged, but then realized Laurie's eyes were still closed. "I think what my mother says makes sense. It's just medicine for my nerves, nothing weird or whatever."

"Okay." Laurie put her arm across her eyes, indicating that the conversation was over.

A couple minutes later, Stacy and Brandy came down with four bottles of beer and handed Laurie and me ours. Then Stacy opened the baggie and handed each of us a tiny piece of paper. Brandy and Laurie were right, they did look like little stickers or tattoos.

"Okay, just put it on your tongue and let it melt," Stacy stuck her tongue out, dropped the LSD on it and kept it out for demonstration. Brandy and Laurie followed suit, keeping their tongues out, too. I thought they looked stupid.

"Go ahead, Dora, we're waiting for you," Stacy prompted.

I carefully placed the paper on my tongue but then shut my mouth. It wasn't long before it turned into a jelly-like blob and then melted away. I opened my beer and took a sip. Stacy was right, it was bitter.

Stacy turned on the stereo and found a good radio station. They all started dancing. I was pretty nervous, so I just sat on the couch and stared at the wall. I was starting to think it wasn't doing anything to me. I was tired and really just wanted to go home and go to bed. All of a sudden, though, my heart started to beat really fast and I felt a wave of warmth wash over me.

I looked up at my friends, because I had been staring at a picture on the wall and not paying any attention to them. Stacy and Laurie were still dancing and Brandy was sprawled out on the floor laughing her ass off. I noticed for the first time how tall and skinny they were.

"Hey, you guys should play basketball," I said, but I didn't even recognize my own voice and they all just ignored me. I looked down at my feet and noticed they were really far away. I looked up, afraid I was going to hit my head on the ceiling, but that way looked normal.

I decided to lay down. I shut my eyes and felt a little bit like I was floating. The music shut off abruptly and I opened my eyes to see Stacy put in a cassette in the player. A new song blared out of the speakers.

"Woo hoo! This is my jam. I loved this song when I was a kid," Brandy tried to get up, but couldn't, so she rolled on the floor laughing until Laurie helped her up. I shut my eyes again and listened to the song.

I remembered it, too, from when I was a little kid, but couldn't remember exactly where I had heard it. I screwed my eyes shut tight and tried to remember. I kept almost remembering and then it would slip away.

But there was one thing I knew for certain, the song was playing once when something really bad happened. I had no idea what it was and wasn't even sure that I wanted to know.

I stood up feeling a little wobbly but knowing I needed to get out of there. Stacy seemed to notice me for the first time since we took the acid when I put on my coat and slung my backpack over my shoulder, "What are you doing, Dora?" I barely recognized her voice either and the song was amplified in my head so it came out very quiet. I wasn't even sure I heard her correctly.

"I'm going home."

"Why?"

"Because I want to."

"Don't you want to stay and party with us?" When Brandy said the word "party" it seemed long and dragged out. I could have just asked Stacy to turn the song off. I knew that would make me feel better, but I couldn't. I had to get away from it. I knew it would echo all night and never stop as long as I stayed there.

"No, I have to go."

"Come on, Dora," Brandy drawled. "Dance with us."

"Nope."

"Why do you have to go?" Stacy asked.

I looked at them for what seemed like an hour. "Because honestly, I don't even really like you guys."

I rushed up the stairs. I didn't have to look at them to know they were all standing there staring at me with their mouths open. Nobody, and I mean nobody talked to Stacy like that. I had to get away from that song, as far away as I could. When I got to the top of the stairs I went through the door and slammed it behind me. I could still hear it. I rushed across the kitchen and out the door and I could still hear it.

I ran across the yard trying to distance myself from it and I could still hear it. Even when I was far enough away that there was no way I could, I still heard it. It was seared in my brain. I didn't want to think about the song. I didn't want to hear it. It made me remember something about my brother Tommy. I wasn't sure what it was, I only knew it was something bad. Something wicked bad.

As soon as I got home, I went right to bed and fell asleep. My mother was already in bed and she had said I could skip my medicine that night anyway, so I wasn't worried about her catching me and knowing I was on drugs.

I put my mixtape into my Walkman so I could listen to different songs and forget that other one. My friends and I were into heavy metal, but my favorite songs from all the different bands were their power ballads, not that I would admit that to anyone.

I had made the tape of all my favorite songs from bands like Ozzy, Def Leppard, and Motley Crüe by waiting near the radio and pressing record when a song I liked came on. Since they were like all kind of gentle, it worked and I was able to fall asleep.

When I woke up in the morning, I still kind of felt like I was tripping and the words to the song came rushing back to me. Mom was surprised to see me home but didn't ask what happened. I think she was just glad I didn't stay at Stacy's, probably she was afraid I would do drugs or something.

Later on in the day I couldn't take it anymore. A verse from the song played over and over in my head and different music or talking to my mother didn't stop it. After lunch I rode my bike to the library and asked the librarian to help me find the song. I wasn't sure who sang it but could guess the title from the verse that was stuck in my head.

The librarian knew right away, led me to the cassettes and handed me an older AC/DC tape. I used my library card to take it out and then rode my bike home. I closed myself up in my room and got it cued up on my stereo with my finger on the play button, afraid to press it. After a while I got up the nerve and did. The song started blaring out of the speakers. Probably too loud.

Mom was in the next room laying down.

She had a migraine.

The house was small.

The walls were thin.

None of that mattered though, because I was not there.

1976

I am eight years old. I am standing in the attic, in front of the window that looks out over the triangle part of the back porch roof. I am in my flannel nightie, barefoot, roused from sleep by some racket on the roof and the loud music, some song about a highway to hell. The attic window is open and a cold gust of wind comes in, blowing my hair around. I can smell my brothers' cigarette smoke.

I hear someone scream, "Get her the fuck out of here!" Somebody grabs me. I can't see who. Then I can't see anything. Somebody's hands are over my eyes as they drag me down the stairs and through the hallway. Rough hands push me inside my room.

"What did you see? Did you see anything?" someone screams in my face. Someone I didn't know. Someone who I should know. Who was it? A boy? A man? He pushes me onto my bed.

"Nothing," I cry. "I didn't see nothing!"

"Go back to sleep. You're having a bad dream."

The song faded out in my memory, and at mine and Mom's winter rental.

When I came back to reality, I was sitting in my desk chair gripping the armrests so hard I left fingernail marks in the wood. My clothes were sticking to me and my hair was damp with sweat.

I turned down the volume on my stereo, grabbed a towel and wiped the sweat from my face. As soon as I caught my breath and my heart didn't feel like it was going to burst right out of my chest, I rewound the tape and started the song again. This time I tried to relax and keep myself grounded in my desk chair. I listened to the song, pressed stop, rewound it, and listened to it again. I listened to it over and over. I didn't allow myself to slip back into my memory.

When I could listen to the whole song without flipping out, I got up and changed my sweat soaked shirt. I peeked in on Mom, who was fully dressed and laying on top of her covers, totally crashed out. Then I went into the bathroom, where I splashed cold water on my face and leaned my head over to drink out of the faucet.

Back in my bedroom, I got comfortable in my chair and played "Highway to Hell" again for the hundredth time. I let myself slip back into the memory. I tried my hardest to stay calm, but the same thing happened. I panicked. I was not fourteen-year-old Dora, sitting in her room, hearing "Highway to Hell" on her stereo.

I was eight-year-old Dora, standing in the attic, freezing and scared to death, hearing about how the singer was playing in a rockin' band and on his way to the promised land, from Tommy's room at the bottom of the attic stairs. When I was asked if I saw something, I lied. I did see something.

Fourteen-year-old Dora cannot see what eight-year-old Dora saw, though. It was too scary, even for her.

Fourteen-year-old Dora cannot, will not, must not, ever see what eight-year-old Dora saw, because if she did, it would destroy her entire world.

I was totally freaked out, not only by what I could remember, but by what I couldn't remember. I put the tape back into its case and rode back to the library to return it. I made a vow that I would never listen to that song again. Whatever it was that had happened that day on the roof was something I didn't want to know.

I tried my hardest to forget the image of me standing in the attic, but it kept coming back to me to haunt me when I least expected it. The very next day I was sitting in class listening to Mr. Thompson's lecture about the proper way to structure an essay and found myself tumbling back into the memory. I was sitting in a warm classroom, obviously fully dressed, and suddenly I was overcome by a chill as though I was barefoot and standing in front of an open window breathing in gulps of cigarette smoke.

"… the last sentence of the first paragraph?"

"Get her the fuck out of here!"

"What did you see? Did you see anything?"

"Dora, can you answer the question?"

"Go back to sleep."

"Hello? Dora?"

"Go back to sleep, you're having a bad dream."

"Get her the fuck…"

"Dora! Do you know the answer or not?"

"I'm sorry, Mr. Thompson. What was the question again?"

The other problem I had, which I wouldn't have considered a problem before, was that I began to be bombarded by other memories as well. It was as though there had been a dam in my brain that had been sealed up. The song I heard that day Stacy's basement had opened a floodgate and the memories began to flow without any control or consent from me.

The next memories that came to me in vivid detail were the day of Tommy's funeral and the weeks following it. I swore that I had absolutely no recollection of what had happened back then prior to hearing that song, but then one day while walking home from the bus stop, a funeral procession went by me, and it all came back to me in an instant:

1976

I put on a striped sundress, but because it is cold out I wear a sweater over it. I wear my Mommy's big floppy hat that has flowers all around the top. The last things I put on are my Wonder Woman knee-high socks and my gym sneakers.

"Ma, make her change. She looks like an idiot!" yells Donny.

"Leave her alone. She's fine," Mommy says before she even sees me.

A ton of people come to the house after the funeral and everyone wants to hug me and talk to me. I am pretty freaked out because I don't even know most of them. It is really quiet, even though the house is full.

People sit in groups whispering and eating little sandwiches. My mother sits on the couch with her hands folded in her lap, staring straight ahead. People go over to her and hug her and talk to her, but she acts like she doesn't even hear them. She moves like a robot and doesn't answer anyone. She just nods her head and grips her hands together in her lap.

I do my best to stay invisible. If one more stranger hugs me I am going to scream. I walk quietly by people and hear things people say that confuse me, but I figure I can sort them out later.

After almost everyone leaves, my Auntie Ginny goes upstairs with Mommy to help her settle down for a nap. Daddy tells me and my brothers to clean up the mess. Jim stays in the kitchen and stacks casseroles that people brought for us into the freezer. Pat, Donny, and I pick up paper plates and cups from the dining room.

When the dining room is clean, I want to go upstairs to my room, but my brothers make me stay downstairs and watch TV with them. Mommy and Daddy are locked up in their room and my brothers say I can't go upstairs because I will disturb them.

They let me choose the shows we watch, which has never happened before. I want to think about what I heard some of the visitors saying, but my brothers don't give me a minute. I heard a bunch of words that I don't know. I have a dictionary I got from school and my favorite hobby is learning the meaning of new words. Two words I had overheard were "non- consensual" and "statutory".

I don't get to look them up because my brothers keep me in the living room into the night, letting me choose whatever we watch and talking to me whenever my eyes move away from the TV.

At dinnertime Jim heats up a casserole. He brings plates upstairs to Mommy and Daddy and the rest of us eat in the TV room. Even after dinner, when I know shows they like are on, they still let me watch my shows. I am confused by the way they are treating me, but I ignore it and enjoy all the attention they are giving me.

My brothers don't even make me go to bed. I fall asleep on the couch. When I wake up in the morning, I am in my bed. I open my eyes and the first thing I see is Jim, sitting in my desk chair watching me sleep.

"Good morning, Sunshine!" he exclaims, using my mother's pet name for me.

"Hi." What is he doing in my room? I didn't want him in there.

For a very long time after the funeral, my brothers never leave me alone. They take me out with them when they go to movies or to the park to shoot hoops, or out to eat, even if they are bringing a girl. Mommy and Daddy are being kind of weird. Mommy stays shut up in her room most of the time, and Daddy leaves early for work and comes back late.

My brothers become my parents, and I love it. Mommy never cooks anymore and my brothers don't know how. So, when all of the casseroles are gone, we start to order out for dinner every night. We have pizza or subs for every meal. My brothers never send me to bed.

Just like the day of the funeral, I fall asleep on the couch and when I wake up in the morning, I am in my room. Every morning one of them is in there, waking me up and telling me to hurry and go into the bathroom to get ready for school, or if it was a weekend or vacation, to hang out with them. By the time I get the chance to look up the words in the dictionary, I have forgotten what they even were.

One Saturday Jim takes me to go skating at the rink where my brothers play hockey. I'm not very good, so Jim skates behind me, holding me under my arms.

Some boy skates by us real fast and shouts, "What's the matter, Jim-Bo? Can't find a good fuck your own age?" A couple seconds later we skate by that same boy who is pinned up against the wall by another boy.

"Lay off, you idiot. That's his little sister. Their brother just killed himself, and she's barely hanging on."

I look back at Jim to see if he knows what that boy is talking about. "Turn around, Dora. You always have to look straight ahead when you're skating, so you don't bump into anybody."

I am really confused. What does that boy mean by, "She's barely hanging on?" Of course, I am sad about my brother, but I'm not having any kind of problems. Is that what my brothers are telling everybody about why I was always with them? They tell me it is because our parents are very sad and they have to help take care of me.

I decide not to worry about it. I am having fun, and to me, that is all that counts.

Chapter 3

1982

For the first couple months of ninth grade, I begged off going to my father's. I said I had too much homework. I had a project due, I had a big test, whatever I could say to get out of going. It wasn't that I didn't want to see my Dad or my brothers, but I was nervous about it.

Even though I couldn't make any sense of my memory about standing in the attic in my nightgown, I had a strange feeling about my brothers that I couldn't identify, and felt it was best that I avoided them for as long as I could, at least until I could figure out what had happened that night.

The homework excuse seemed absolutely reasonable to my parents, after all it was my first year of high school, the first year that actually counted. The funny thing was, when I started using homework and studying as an excuse to not go to my father's, I actually began to do really well in school. My first quarter report card was all A's. I wasn't ever what anybody would call a poor student, but I never got straight A's before.

I also discovered that totally immersing myself in my studies was what I had to do to turn off, or at the very least slow down, the flow of memories. Even though I used to say that I wished I had more memories about my brother, that wasn't the case now. I was pretty sure that I didn't want to remember anything at all. In fact, I wanted to forget the things that I had already remembered.

On the outside, of course, it looked like I was doing terrific. My teachers were thrilled about my grades. My parents were ecstatic. I was invited to join the honor society at school and I accepted. I figured it was a good way to keep myself busy. My whole family came to the induction ceremony. Pat even came from off-Island to go. I also went out for the basketball team. My brothers were happy about that. They had all been basketball stars in high school and figured I could continue their legacy.

I was a very good basketball player and became a starter for the Varsity team, even though I was only a freshman. Everyone had always assumed that I would play. I had never had any intention to do it before, but now it made for a nice distraction. After spending the entire school day paying attention to my teachers, doing activities for the honor society, going to basketball practice or off-Island for a game, and doing my homework, I was too tired to remember anything.

I found myself hanging out with a new crowd of friends, too. My old friends weren't really into sports or school, and besides, since I told them I didn't like them they didn't even try to talk to me, and I totally avoided them. One day I was at my locker, getting a notebook I had forgotten. Class had already started, so the halls were empty. I was digging through my locker and not paying attention to anything around me, when I felt a tap on my shoulder. It was a little too rough to be mistaken for a friendly gesture.

"What's going on, Dora?" Stacy's voice was heavy with sarcasm.

I closed my locker and turned around, scanning the halls for a teacher, anyone. No such luck, so I settled my gaze on Stacy, Brandy, and Laurie, who didn't look like they were all that happy to see me. "Nothing much. How are you guys?"

"Fine. Fine. We're all doing just fine, Dora. But we're wondering about you. We haven't seen you in a while."

"And I've called you like a million times and you never answer," Laurie complained.

"Yeah, I know, I've been pretty busy. You know how it is…."

"No, actually we don't know how it is, Dora. Why don't you tell us?" Brandy piped in.

"I've just had a lot to do. Homework and stuff."

"Oh, and don't forget basketball. Heard you made the team. Congratulations." Stacy was not saying that to be nice.

I pretended like I didn't notice though and decided sarcasm would be my best defense. "Thanks, it's fun. You know, Stacy, you should try out for a sport. I hear the cheerleaders are a pretty nice group of girls. You should get along good with them." Nobody liked the cheerleaders and my old friends knew I was being facetious.

"Wow, that's fucked up," Laurie said.

"No, you want to know what's really fucked up? When somebody goes and totally blows off their friends. I mean, when's the last time we saw you? Oh, that's right, when you told us you didn't even like us." Stacy looked back at Brandy and Laurie, who nodded like the little groupies they were, totally under her control. Stacy put both of her hands on my shoulders and shoved me into the lockers. "We don't appreciate being ignored."

"Dora!" a voice rang out from down the hall. "Mr. Harman is wondering what's taking you so long."

I looked up and saw Olivia walking toward us. She had been my best friend when we were little kids and she was on the basketball team with me. She obviously said that to save me. We weren't even in class together. I didn't even have Mr. Harman as a teacher.

Stacy poked me in the chest with her dragon-lady fingernail. "See you around, Culligan." Then she, Brandy, and Laurie hurried down the hall, laughing.

"What was that all about?" Olivia reached my locker. "I thought you were friends with them?"

"Not anymore, I guess." My heart was still thumping in my ears.

"I never understood why you hung out with them, anyway. They're not very nice. You're nothing like them."

I laughed. "I guess I'll take that as a compliment."

"I don't know if I'd go that far," Olivia said with a nervous little laugh. "You just aren't a bitch like they are, at least you never were."

Olivia started down the hall the way she had been heading. "Well, thanks for rescuing me, anyway," I called out to her.

"No problem, Culligan. And hey, I'll see you at practice."

1970s

Olivia is the first best friend I have, who I don't hang out with because our mothers are friends. We are in the same kindergarten class and our cubbies are side-by-side. On the first day of school, Donald steals my snack while we are walking to school and eats it, so Olivia shares hers with me. The next day I bring extra and share it with her. We become best friends.

In kindergarten and first grade we don't play after school or on the weekends. By second grade we are old enough to ask our parents about playing together, and we go to each other's houses at least once a week. In third grade we start having sleepovers. Everybody in my house loves Olivia, and she loves them. My father nicknames her "Olive Oyl" from the Popeye cartoon because she is tall and skinny. Well, not that tall and skinny, but taller and skinnier than me.

We have a huge basement in our house that my dad calls a rec room. We have a pool table and a ping-pong table and a basketball net attached to one of the posts that holds the house up. I always want to go down there and play, but I am too afraid to go by myself because the light switch is halfway down the stairs and it is really dark down there with no lights.

I follow my brothers whenever they go down there. They complain to my mother, saying that I am bugging them, but she tells them to quit their whining and stop being selfish; the basement is as much mine to enjoy as it is theirs, so they let me follow them down, but then they get me out of there pretty quick.

Everyone starts doing something and then one of my brothers would shout, "Look! A mouse!" or "Oh my God! I just saw a bat!" I would go running upstairs and wouldn't go back down for the rest of the night. At first, they would do something mean, like throw a ball at me, or trip me, but then I would just tell my mother and she would make them come upstairs. It didn't take them long to figure out that creepy crawly things were the way to get rid of me, and there was nothing for me to tell on them to get them in trouble.

The only exception to this is whenever Olivia sleeps over; they let us follow them down there and don't try to pull their mouse or bat stunt. Probably because with two of us there, they figure their trick won't work. It doesn't matter to me, because I have more fun down there when Olivia is over anyway. We usually play ping-pong while they shoot pool or practice basketball.

One night when Olivia sleeps over we get in a big fight. I want my mother to take her home, but I know her parents went out and my mother would just tell me no anyway. She would tell me that a good hostess always finds a way to make things right for a guest, so I didn't even ask. Instead I sulk and try to make Olivia's night as miserable as she is making mine.

It all starts when we go down to the rec room. I get the ping pong paddles and am ready to play, but Olivia wouldn't come. She wants to play pool with my brothers. I sit on the steps and watch them teach her how to hold a pool stick and about the rules of the game. The longer it goes on, the madder I get. She never stops playing with them the whole time we are down there. By the time my mother calls us upstairs to go to bed, I am so mad I want to scream. When we go into my room after brushing our teeth and changing into our nighties, I tell Olivia that she has to sleep on the floor.

"That's not how it's supposed to be," she informs me, as if I didn't already know. "The guest is supposed to get to sleep on the bed!"

"Not tonight," I snap at her. "And if you don't like it, you can go home."

I get in my bed and pull the covers over my head. I don't even give her a pillow and blankets. I work so hard at ignoring Olivia that I don't even notice when she leaves. After a while I turn over to say something to her and she is gone.

I get up and check the bathroom, figuring she must be in there, but it is empty. I head down the hall towards my brothers' rooms. Jim and Pat are out somewhere in Jim's new car and Donny is having his own sleepover at his friend's house, so I check Tommy's room, knowing he is the only one home.

His door is closed and I push it open without knocking, breaking what my mother calls her "Golden Rule." Olivia is laying in his bed under the covers and he is sitting on the edge. He jumps up when he sees me in the doorway.

"I'm telling Mommy!" I yell.

"We weren't doing anything, Dora!" he shouts.

I don't know what he is talking about, why he says they aren't doing anything. "She's my friend and you guys have been having her play with you all night! It's not fair! And now you even have her hanging out with you in here!"

"What do you expect, Dora? You weren't even letting her sleep on the bed! She just came in here to lie down for a little while. You were totally ignoring her and making her sleep on the floor without even giving her a pillow or blankets!"

"I don't care! I'm still telling!"

"Don't, Dora. Go on, Olivia. Go back to Dora's room and she'll let you sleep on the bed. You be a 'good hostess' now, Dora. You hear me? Or I'm gonna be the one who tells Mom on you."

Olivia and I go back into my room. I let her sleep on the bed. I am afraid Tommy is going to tell mother I was not being a good hostess.

After that night, even though we still play in school, Olivia doesn't want to come over to my house anymore.

Chapter 4

1982

Olivia and I were friends until seventh grade. Like so many other kids who grow away from their childhood friends when they go to junior high, we started hanging around with different groups of kids and drifted apart. She had joined the "Student/Jock" crowd and I guess I was kind of in the "Preppie" group. My friends and I sat around and painted our nails and talked about fashion and hairstyles.

We kept magazines hidden inside of our books and passed notes to each other when we were supposed to be studying. We teased girls who didn't meet our fashion stand. We had no interest in being nice to other people, getting good grades, or getting sweaty on the courts or fields of The Martha's Vineyard Regional High School Sports and Recreational Program.

Now that I had joined the basketball team and found myself sidling in on her group of friends, Olivia and I rekindled our friendship, as if we had not spent the last two years acting like we didn't know each other existed.

I decided that if there was anyone I was going to talk about my memory with, it would be Olivia. She knew Tommy and she was my friend when he died. As much as I would have liked to convince myself that throwing myself into my studies and keeping myself so busy would make me forget, it just put a hold on things. It allowed me to function day-to-day, but it didn't eradicate the memory. It had come, and now it was here to stay.

I invited Olivia over after basketball practice one day and she was surprised when we got off the bus on Barnes Road. "This is where you live?" she asked. "Your house..?"

"Oh, you didn't hear? My parents are putting it up for sale. They're getting a divorce."

"Really?" she asked, incredulous. "Wow, they always seemed so happy to me. I go by your road all the time. I had no idea you didn't live there anymore."

When we got inside, Mom was already home and was surprised to see Olivia. "Olive Oyl! How are you?"

"I'm good, Mrs. Culligan. How about you?"

"I'm doing just fine. So, what are you girls up to?"

"We're just gonna go in my room and study. We have a killer algebra test tomorrow."

"Well, go on then, and I'll make you some nachos. You still eat them, right, Olive Oyl?"

"Yours, definitely, Mrs. C."

When we were all settled in my room with our algebra books open and our notes spread out all over the place, I decided to just ask her. "How much do you remember about being a kid?"

"I don't know. Not too much, I guess. Sometimes I think I remember stuff, but then I realize I don't actually remember it. It's pictures of it that I remember. Why?"

Maybe if she had admitted that she remembered stuff I would have continued, but I changed my mind. I decided I just wasn't ready to talk about it. "No reason really. I was just wondering, you know."

"So, are we going to study or what?"

We worked on a few problems and then Mom came in with the nachos. "I didn't make too much. I don't want you girls to spoil your dinner. Are you staying to eat, Olive Oyl?"

"No, thank you, Mrs. Culligan. Mom is expecting me home."

"Oh, okay, then. Well, maybe next time. Dora, make sure you share." When Mom left the room Olivia and I looked at each other and cracked up. She obviously thought we were still seven.

We went through the formulas we knew we were going to be tested on and then made our "cheat sheets." Our teacher didn't make us memorize formulas because she said no mathematician would ever have to sit and use a formula from memory. She thought it was more important that we learned how to use the formulas correctly, than wasting our time memorizing them. She let us bring one sheet of paper with as many formulas and notes as we could fit on it. We still had to study though, because if we didn't know how to use the formulas, having them in front of us would have done us no good.

Olivia's mother came to pick her up at six thirty and Mom called me into the kitchen to have dinner.

"What's cooking?" I asked.

"Pork chops," Mom put my plate in front of me. "It was nice to see Olivia. I didn't think you two were friends anymore."

"She's on the basketball team, so we've been hanging out," I explained, pushing goopy mashed potatoes around on my plate.

"That's nice. I like her much better than those other girls you were friends with."

"Yeah, I know. As soon as we get her off heroin and stop prostituting, I think she'll be a good influence on me." My mother looked at me. She was pretty used to my sarcasm, but since I always said my sarcastic remarks straight, it was hard to tell if I was being serious. "Ma, you haven't seen her since she was seven years old. You have no idea what she's like now."

"So, she's not really...?" Mom asked.

"No, I was kidding. She really is a good kid. You just act like you know all about her, just because you knew her years ago. People change. I'm sure Stacy was a sweet little girl, too."

Mom laughed. "You'll understand someday, Dora. Mothers just know certain things."

Really, Mom? Because it seemed to me lately like there might have been an awful lot of things you didn't know.

Toward the end of October, Mom had a date. With Dad. She called me into her room when I got home from school and I was flabbergasted to see every outfit she owned strewn all over her room.

"What's going on?" I asked.

"I have a date with your father and I can't find anything to wear. Here, help me."

"Mom, it really doesn't matter what you wear," I said, as though I was talking to a little kid. "Dad has seen all of your clothes. He probably bought them or was there when you bought them."

Mom flopped back on her bed. "Oh my, you're right." Then she sat up. "Get your jacket. We're leaving."

"Where are we going?"

"To Lillian's. I need to get a new outfit to wear."

We went to Vineyard Haven and I swear Mom tried on everything they had. She was acting like she was going out on a first date. "I don't get you, Mom," I said when we were back in the car on our way home, a dress that wasn't any different than the ones she already had folded in a box on my lap. "I mean, you're married to the guy, what's the big deal?"

She mumbled something about me not understanding, and when we got home she went to get ready. She made me help her curl her hair and put on her make-up.

"How did this whole date thing come up, anyway?" I asked as I sprayed about a thousand pounds of hairspray onto the curls we ironed into her hair to keep them in place.

"He mailed a letter asking me if I wanted to go out for dinner."

"How do you know it's a date, then? Maybe he wants to talk about the divorce or about selling the house or something."

"Nope. It's definitely a date," she replied with a dreamy smile on her lips.

"Yeah?" I asked. "And how do you know that?"

"Because he did the exact same thing to me as he did when he asked me out for the first time."

"Are you serious?"

"I am," she said.

"Okay, what did he say, then?"

"It's not what he said. It's what he did."

"What did he do?" I asked. "Or do I not want to know?"

"We were taking Shakespeare together for our college English requirement, and he passed me a note in class one day."

"What? A note asking you out?"

"When have you ever known your father to be so mundane? He gave me a list of Shakespeare's sonnets, with line numbers and word numbers. Then I had to go through the sonnets and find the words. It spelled out 'Mayst thine self desire to honour me with thy presence?'"

"You're kidding right?"

"Nope. This time, he did with a book he knew that I had read. He mailed me a letter with the title of the book, then the page numbers, the paragraph, and the number of the word, and this time it spelled out 'Will you at honor me with your company on the 23rd day of October at the Ocean View?'"

Mom was sitting on the toilet lid while I was doing her hair. "Please, get up," I pulled on her arm. "I've got to puke right now."

Mom laughed at me, but she got up and checked herself in the mirror. I opened the toilet lid and pretended to puke.

She laughed again. "What's so bad about that? I think it was sweet."

"Yeah, nauseatingly sweet. So, what are you guys gonna do? Get back together?"

"I'm not really sure. I guess we'll just take it one step at a time, see how things go."

"Do you even want to get back with him?"

"I love you father and I miss him very much."

"Jeez, Mom, all you guys ever did was fight," I said.

"I'm not saying we don't have some problems we need to work out, everyone does. Marriage isn't easy, Dora. You'll find out someday when you get married."

"No thanks. If it's anything like yours and Dad's, I think I'll stay single. Maybe I'll marry a gay guy who wants to keep it in the closet and get artificially inseminated. That way, everybody will be happy."

Mom laughed again and then turned to face me. "Okay, I'm ready. How do I look?"

"Exactly the same way you did the day you got married, except without the wedding gown and veil."

"Come on, Dora. I'm serious," Mom scolded, her hands on her hips.

"Seriously, Mom, you look good. I think he might even ask you out on a second date."

Mom obviously had a great time on her date because she came home really late. I was half-asleep on the couch waiting for her and when she opened the door, I jumped up. "Where have you been, young lady? I've been waiting for you! The least you could have done was called!"

Mom broke out in a fit of giggles and we plopped down on the couch together. She rested her head on my lap. "Oh, darling, he was a perfect gentleman! I think he just might be the man I'll marry!"

"Just as long as you don't mention anything to him about your first marriage," I said.

Dad asked Mom out for another date on Halloween. Mom wasn't sure if she should go out or not because our new neighborhood had a lot of houses and seemed like it would be very busy with trick-or-treaters. A lot of our neighbors even decorated their yards. There weren't many houses on our old street so hardly anybody came to the house. Most years Mom took me around the neighborhood and Dad stayed home to give out candy, in case anyone did come.

"Mom," I said to her, "I'll stay here and pass out candy. You go out with Dad, it's not a problem."

"What about you? Don't you plan on going out?" she asked.

I had already decided that I was too old to trick-or-treat, even though some of my friends were going out and invited me. "I planned on just staying home anyway and watching a movie. Carrie is on."

"If you're sure…" Mom began.

"It's fine," I interrupted. "Just leave the candy out, I have a feeling we'll get a lot of customers."

I snuggled on the couch with a blanket from my bed and watched Carrie, in between having to get up and answer the door to give out the mini candy bars my mother had bought. I thought about the first time I had watched that movie – when I was maybe six or seven - it was kind of the same way- in bits and pieces.

My mother had let Jim watch it in her room, because she didn't want any of us younger kids to see it. Jim let me sneak in and watch it with him, but every time I heard a creak or the wind blew, I would think it was Mom coming, so I would run back to my room. I barely even got the plot back then, so I wasn't scared.

During the scene when Carrie was getting crowned as prom queen, the doorbell rang for like the hundredth time. I grabbed the bowl of candy and answered the door but kept my eyes mostly on the TV because I knew Carrie was about to get a bucket of pig's blood dumped on her and I didn't want to miss it.

"Excuse me, the bowl is empty." I looked away from the television and into the eyes of a little girl who was dressed in a costume that seemed awfully familiar.

"Are you supposed to be Raggedy Anne?" I asked, because the color of the dress was right, and her wig was red, but none of it looked quite right.

"No, I'm Madeline. Who is Raggedy Anne?"

"Never mind," I said, reaching for the second bowl Mom had left "just in case." She grabbed a handful of mini candy bars.

"Thank you! Happy Halloween!" she called as she skipped away to meet up with the rest of her group at the end of the driveway.

I put the bowl down and snuggled back on the couch. Carrie was officially on her murderous rampage, but I barely even saw it.

1975

My brothers want to take me out to trick-or-treat. Mommy gives them a ton of directions about keeping an eye on me and making sure I don't walk in the road. I'm not totally sure, but I don't think she trusts them not to take off with their friends and leave me, because she keeps telling them over and over not to do it. In the end, she decides to trust them, I think because she is glad that she doesn't have to take me. I sure don't trust them, but I guess I am safe as long as Tommy is there.

My mother made my costume, and it is perfect. I look exactly like Raggedy Anne, who is my favorite, next to Winnie-the-Pooh. Mommy even put make-up on me to give me Raggedy Anne's rosy cheeks and freckles. My brothers take me over to a neighborhood on the other side of the school, even though my mother tells them we are not supposed to cross the big road.

They tell me they heard the people across town give out full sized candy bars, so I go without too much complaining. My mother's rules are usually very important to me and I try to never break them, but my brothers tell me to come with them or else they are just going to take me home and I would skip trick-or-treating that year.

Even though I am nervous about crossing the big road, it really does seem like the people over there give out better candy and Donny keeps checking his watch to make sure we head home on time so we will be there at exactly eight o'clock, which is when our mother told them to have me home.

Besides, they do watch me and make sure I stay out of the road. They also meet up with a couple groups of their friends and don't leave me. When we start to walk home I am relieved. I hadn't realized how worried I had been all night that they were going to do something mean to me.

When we get near my school, which is right across from the graveyard, I hear Jim shout, "Go! Go!" and turn around just in time to see him tackle Tommy to the ground. Pat and Donny grab me by the arms and pull me into the graveyard. They know I am afraid to go through there because I wouldn't take it as a shortcut when it was light out. On our way home it is full dark and I am scared to death.

I scream, "Let go of me!" but they won't. They just drag me deeper and deeper into the graveyard. Even if they had let me go then, I would never be able to find my way back to the road and would be lost with dead people all around me. They finally stop and let go of my arms. They are breathing heavily and they both drop to the ground, rolling around and laughing. We are near some kind of a shed that I have never seen before and I have no idea where we are.

"Get up and take me home right now, you jerks!" I scream at them.

"Relax, Dora, it's no big deal. We just needed to take this short-cut to get home on time," Pat says.

"Where's Tommy?" I shout. "I want Tommy!"

"We're just going to wait here for him and Jim. They'll be here in a minute," Donny replies.

I sit down on the ground and lean against the shed. I squeeze my hands between my legs to stop myself from peeing in my costume. I hear Tommy yell my name from far away and start to yell back, but Pat clamps his hand over my mouth. "Shh, Dora, don't yell. That's how the dead people wake up."

"Hey," Donny says loud enough to scare me that he was going to wake them up. That was something my mother always said – Dora, you're being too loud. You'll wake the dead – so I totally believe it could happen. "Do you know what this shed is for, Pat?"

"I have no clue," Pat says.

"It's where they store the dead people when the ground is frozen and they can't bury them."

"It's frozen now, huh?" Pat asks.

"Sure it is. Right after Labor Day it starts to freeze. That's why the summer people leave then. They're afraid the water will freeze, too and they won't be able to get off-Island to their regular houses."

"Is that a fact?" Pat inquires.

"It sure is! I heard all about it and I heard there's three dead people in there right now!"

"Stop it!" I holler, jumping to my feet to get away from the shed.

Pat grabs my arm. "Don't be afraid, Dora. He's lying. He's just trying to scare you."

As Pat talks to me, I don't notice Donny opening the door to the shed. Then he shouts, "Now!"

Pat pulls me over to the shed and pushes me inside. "Go see for yourself, but if there are coffins in there, don't scream or you'll wake them up, and they can get out!" Then he slams the door shut. I put my hands over my mouth to trap in my scream and then I do it – I pee in my costume.

I start feeling around to find the door. I hear clanking noises and then a skeleton reaches out and grabs my shoulder. I can't help it, I scream, but it doesn't even matter since at least one of them is already awake.

The door opens and Tommy reaches in and grabs my arm, pulling me out. I look back and by the light of his flashlight I see what is in there: lawnmowers, rakes, and shovels. I see the plastic rake that had fallen – the skeleton that grabbed me just before Tommy opened the door. Jim, Pat, and Donny take off ahead of us and we can hear them laughing in the distance.

Tommy yells at them for a while and they yell back that I am a baby and can't take a joke, they were only fooling around with me.

Then he talks to me, "Dead people don't ever wake up, no matter what, not even on Halloween. If they did, don't you think you would have seen at least one? Have you ever seen a dead person walking around?"

"I guess not," I whisper because my throat hurts from screaming.

When we get home, Mom is in the sitting room reading a book and doesn't even look up, which is good because I don't want her to see that I ripped my costume and peed in it. My rules for that night had only been two: to listen to my brothers and not ruin my costume.

"Run upstairs and get your nightie on and then bring your candy to Daddy so he can check it."

I go to the bathroom and wash my legs and then I hide my costume at the bottom of the mess in my closet.

My father is really funny on Halloween. Every year he dumps my candy on the dining room table and goes through it, saying he is looking for poison and razor blades.

"Hmm, there's a razor blade in this one," he said, and by the time he finished going through my candy he would have a pile of candy that he liked.

I know he is just teasing me; none of the candy have razor blades. He just wants to take the candy he likes. I don't mind because we don't have the same taste in candy anyway. He likes dark chocolate and stuff with coconut in it.

I giggle every time he says he finds candy that has been "tampered with" and that year, by the time he is done, I am laughing so hard I forgot all about what happened in the graveyard.

Chapter 5

1982

By Thanksgiving, Mom and Dad went on three more dates. They also started going to a marriage counselor to try and figure out what they could do to fix their marriage. They were also talking about going away to some "Marriage Retreat" weekend. I wasn't sure how I felt about the whole thing. Mom didn't seem like she was all that unhappy without Dad in her life.

When I got home from school on the Wednesday before Thanksgiving, Mom and I went to the Vineyard Haven A&P to shop. I was going to be helping her cook by making appetizers. I found three different ones in her cookbooks and made a shopping list of the ingredients. I was also going to make her famous celery stick appetizer. They were stuffed with cream cheese that had chopped olives mixed in it. When we got to the store I went off to get what was on my list while Mom bought everything she needed to make dinner.

That night Mom and I went to sleep at Dad's house, because everyone was coming home and she was going to make dinner. She needed to get up early and start the turkey. When we got to the house, I was relieved because Dad was the only one home. Donny and Pat were already home for Thanksgiving but they were out with their friends. I went upstairs and headed for the baby room across from Dad's. I met Mom in the hallway.

"Oh, honey, could you do me a huge favor and go sleep in your old bedroom? I was going to sleep in here."

"You're not going to sleep in your room?" I asked.

"No, Daddy and I talked about this with Missy, and she thought it might be better if we waited a little longer to bring our relationship to that level."

"Who's Missy?"

"Our marriage counselor."

This lady was actually a marriage counselor? Did they honestly pay her for such stupid advice? They had been married for like twenty years and probably having sex for twenty-five. She thought it would be better if they waited to bring their relationship to that level. She didn't sound like a marriage counselor to me, she sounded like she was pulling a fast one on them. "Okay, sure. Whatever."

I lugged my suitcase down the hall and stood in front of my old bedroom door. It was shut. There was no way I wanted to go in there. I had already decided that I was not going to go anywhere near the attic, but standing in front of the door, I got the feeling I didn't want to go in that room, either. I had no choice, though. What would I tell Mom and Dad?

"Lately I've been having these memories and none of them are good. In fact, I'm pretty sure they're really bad, even though I only have bits and pieces of them. So, I'm getting this feeling that if I go in that room, I'm going to remember something terrible that happened to me in there. Mind if I sleep on the couch?"

Obviously, that wasn't going to work, so I just took a deep breath and opened the door. The room hadn't changed at all from the last time I was in there, when I moved across the hall from my parents' room. The canopy bed, my vanity, everything was still there, except now it was covered with a layer of dust. It also smelled stale, like nobody had been in there for a long time. The rug was just the way I remembered it, so thick and plush I could imagine that it was like what walking on the clouds would feel like.

I threw my suitcase on the bed and opened the window to air it out. I went down to the broom closet and got the vacuum cleaner and the dusting supplies. I cleaned the whole room, then got sheets from the linen closet and made the bed. I unpacked my bag, carefully refolding my clothes and putting them in the bureau drawer. I was keeping myself busy, and I knew why. I was just delaying the inevitable, trying to put off what I knew was waiting for me.

Then I sat down on the bed and let the memory wash over me. I was like a person who had seizures and could tell when it was going to happen, before it happened. It was like I got some "memory aura" or something. I knew the memory was there, pulsing behind my eyes, wanting to come out.

I figured now was as good a time as any to have it. It wasn't like I was going to be able to stop it, if I waited any longer. I had always remembered the first part of the day, when I went shopping with my mother and she bought me a bottle of bubbles, but what happened later just came back to me:

1975

I get in trouble because I spill the bottle of bubbles on my mother's new rug and she sends me to bed early. Usually I don't mind getting sent to my room because I could just read my Richard Scarry books and nobody bothers me. I mind that night though, because Happy Days is on and I never miss it. It is one of the few shows I like that I get to watch, because my brothers like it, too.

I am so mad at my Mommy for making me miss my one favorite show. The only reason why I spilled the bottle was because I blew the most gigantic bubble I had ever seen and I tried to catch it on my wand so I could show it to everybody. I wasn't looking where I was going and I bumped into the table where I left the bottle. I got paper towels and wiped it up. It was almost all the way clean, and my mother never would have known, except Donny sees me and tells her.

Mommy says she isn't punishing me because I had a spill, but because I was playing in her sitting room, and I knew I wasn't supposed to be playing in there, especially with bubbles.

Also, I am in trouble because I didn't tell her I spilled the bubbles and wiped it up to try to hide it from her. I try to tell her I wiped it up to clean it, not hide it, but she won't let me talk. Her sitting room is a really fancy room. My Mommy's special room. Nobody but her ever goes in there, even my Daddy, unless my parents have company.

There is a matching couch and loveseat covered with plastic. There is a coffee table and two tables, one on each side of the couch. The tops of the tables are glass and they have matching lamps on them. The lamps also match the chandelier that hangs in the middle of the room. They all have crystals that hang down and make little rainbows all over the ceiling and walls when the light hits them just right. There is a grandfather clock in there that was passed down in my Mommy's family and that she always says is going to be mine when I grow up.

There is also a piano in there that nobody ever plays. In the corner Mommy has an old- fashioned spinning wheel that she bought at a yard sale and refinished. She crocheted an afghan that matched the couch and loveseat and that she laid over the seat of the wheel. I did know that I wasn't supposed to play in there, but I didn't mean to spill the bubbles, and didn't think I should have been made to miss Happy Days because of it. I read Richard Scarry for a little while and then I shut off my light, snuggle up with my Winnie the Pooh and cry myself to sleep.

I don't know how long after I go to sleep when I wake up again, because of some noise in my room. I sit up in my bed and say, "Who's there?"

Nobody answers me, but then I feel somebody on my bed. I feel a crushing weight and I can't breathe. I taste blood. I want to scream but my mouth won't work. My entire body screams with agony though.

Then I am alone again and I cry for the second time that night, for a reason that is much worse than missing Happy Days

Chapter 6

1982

I got up early the next morning to help Mom get ready for dinner. She wanted me to go up to the attic to get the box of Thanksgiving decorations that were stored up there. I refused.

"Don't even tell me, Dora, that at your age, you're still afraid of the attic and the basement," Dad said, laughing. I just shrugged and Dad sent Donny up to get the box.

When I was a little kid, we always had a half-day of school the Wednesday before Thanksgiving. When I got home, Mom would have me help her by decorating. She had these little dolls that were made out of cornhusks and were dressed like Pilgrims and Indians. She had a little dollhouse banquet table and I would set them up on the credenza, like a little first Thanksgiving. Mom also had a wicker cornucopia and fake fruit that I would organize, too.

When Donny brought the box to me in the dining room, I started setting it all up and it felt kind of nice, familiar somehow. I could focus on that. It was nice for a little while to be able to think about some good memories.

I was starting to get really frustrated with this whole memory thing. It seemed like if I was going to remember something, I should be able to remember it in its entirety. These shadowy, fragmented memories were just making me feel anxious.

After I set up the cornhusk doll Thanksgiving I went into the pantry to get out the holiday dishes. Mom had a set of fancy dishes that we only used on Thanksgiving, Christmas, and Easter. We used regular plates for the rest of the year, but Mom did have different sets to match the season; autumn colored trees and pumpkins for the fall, a snowy scene for the winter, flowers for the spring and summer.

Pat showed up at about eleven o'clock and he went into the TV room to watch football with Dad. I was done setting up the decorations and was making my appetizers while Mom finished making the pies. Jim came at noon time and brought a girl with him. Mom was surprised and not really too happy with him.

"I wasn't aware you were bringing a guest. I wish you had let me know. Your father and I are trying to…" she told him.

"I know, Mom, it's okay," he said, interrupting her. "She's not staying to eat. We just wanted to tell you something and since this is the first time we've all been together in months, we thought this would be a good time."

Jim called everybody into the sitting room. "Mom, Dora, this is Maria. Maria, this is my mom and my little sister Dora. You know everyone else." Maria came over to us and shook our hands, if you could call it that. She actually offered us a limp-wristed hand, as though she expected us to kiss it or something. I was pretty sure she had to be from Edgartown. Whether it was true or not, I didn't know, but we considered people from there to be snooty.

"It's very nice to meet you, Maria," Mom said. "So, what's going on?" As if she couldn't already tell.

"We wanted to let you all know that I've asked Maria to be my wife," Jim answered proudly.

A big burst of excitement ran through the room as Dad got up and patted Jim on the shoulder and my brothers took turns giving him guy hugs, throwing one arm around him and banging him on the back. Mom went over to Maria and gave her a hug. Maria had a huge smile on her face as if she thought she had already won Mom over, but I could tell by Mom's face that her heart just wasn't in it.

Maria stayed and had appetizers with us. Mom asked her a bunch of questions about her and her family. She wasn't even from the Island (one point against her), and neither were her parents (two more points). Her family owned a house that they rented for most of the summer and came to stay themselves for one week in August and vacations like Thanksgiving and Christmas.

And I was exactly right, it was in Edgartown. She and Jim had met in college and had been dating since then. Maria told my mother how she came to the Island to see Jim whenever she could and he went off-Island to see her. Jim never said it, and neither did Maria but I heard my brothers talking about it later - Maria was living with Jim and they also had had an apartment together when they were in college.

"Aren't you going to go over there and tell her parents?" Mom asked right after Maria left.

"We already told them. Last week, when I asked her."

"Oh, so you tell them, and then wait a whole week before telling us? And this is the first time I even meet the girl, when you tell me you're going to marry her?"

"Like I said, we wanted to wait until the whole family was together."

"That's fine. Let's not let it ruin our dinner. It's time to eat." Jim made a face like he didn't understand how his wedding announcement could spoil our dinner, but I understood what Mom was saying. He should have at least introduced her to Mom before he sprang the big news on her.

I already knew that I wasn't going to like her. She was a total fake, and I could see right through her. I also knew that Mom was never going to like her. Nobody would ever be good enough for her precious son.

We went into the dining room to sit down and eat. It was kind of funny how we all gravitated to where we used to sit when we were kids. Dad carved the turkey and then Mom said the Thanksgiving blessing. We all served ourselves and then we played the Thanksgiving game Mom made up when we were kids.

One person started and they had to say something they were thankful for that started with the letter 'A,' the next person with the letter "B," and so on.

Mom started, "Apple pies that come out just right!" Which hers had done.

"Boys," Dad said. "My boys."

Donny went next, "Chimichangas!"

"Donny…" Mom reprimanded.

"I'm serious, Mom! They've gotten me through an awful lot of late night studying sessions!"

Jim had "D" and he said, "Dad."

Pat couldn't let Donny get one over him. "Enchiladas."

"Hmm," Mom said. "I'm sensing a Mexican food theme here. Maybe I should have made tacos instead of turkey!"

"Mexican food. The staple of every all-American college boy's diet," Dad said laughing. "Go ahead, Dora. You have 'F'."

"Forgetfulness," I didn't even hesitate.

Mom laughed. "Why would you be thankful for that? Some days I can't remember my own name! I'm not thankful at all!"

"No reason. I don't know why I said it. It was just the first word that popped into my head," I answered. I wasn't sure, but I thought my brothers may have exchanged a brief look. "I'll change it. Friends. I'm thankful for my friends."

When we finished eating, Dad and my brothers went into the TV room to watch some more football. Mom and I cleaned up the dining room. After we had everything cleaned off the table and put all the leftovers in the fridge, Mom gave me a cloth and some cleaner for the table, then she went into the kitchen to load the dishwasher.

I wiped the table down, getting rid of all the crumbs and spills, and then I polished it and put the placemats back. I put the flower centerpiece back on the table and relit the candles. Mom delivered the little plates to me that were to be used to serve the pies. She made an apple pie, a pumpkin pie, and a pecan pie, which was my favorite.

After I set the table, I plopped down in my seat, glad for a minute to be able to rest my feet. Mom brought in the pies, along with vanilla ice cream and homemade whipped cream, then she called my family in for dessert. My brothers come barreling at the table like they'd never eaten before.

"It's been a long time since we've all eaten together," Mom said after everybody had been served and had started eating their pie. "Why don't we go around the table and everybody can tell us what they've been up to." My brothers all groaned like this was the worst torture ever, as if we didn't do this every single night at dinner when we were growing up.

1975

There is a knock at the door. Mommy is mad that someone is there. It's dinner time, six o'clock, and everyone knows we eat at six, so nobody should be knocking.

Dinner is a very special time in our house. My Mommy sets the table every night the way most people set them only for holidays. We always have fresh flowers on the table and she even lights candles. Nobody is allowed to do anything at the table, like read or do homework. We have to go around and talk about what our day has been like.

On that night, Jim is in the middle of telling us about a boy in his class who got caught cheating on his history test. We had already heard about Pat's basketball practice and this dorky kid who had tried to do a layup but ended up falling when the safety pin that held up his shorts had snapped undone.

My father tells us a story about a man who had an operation and had part of his leg cut off. When he woke up, he was really mad that they got rid of his leg; because of his religion, he thought he would need to save it to get buried with him or he wouldn't go to heaven. Mommy gets mad at Daddy for telling that story, saying it is not appropriate "dinner conversation."

Jim stops talking in the middle of his sentence when there is a knock on the door. My brothers glance at each other, looking worried, because whoever has a friend at the door is going to suffer what they all call "The Wrath of Mom," for daring to let one of their friends come over at dinnertime. I'm not worried that it is one of my friends. They are not allowed out after dark.

My Mommy wipes her face with her napkin and gets up from the table. Her lips are puckered up together in a way that shows she is upset. I can hear her open the door and then I hear voices. I expect that she will come back to the table, sit down in her seat, and continue eating as though the knock never happened. Then later she'll yell at whichever of my four brothers had a friend stop by.

That's not what happens though. She shouts in alarm, though I can't tell what she is saying. Then I hear the pounding of heavy footsteps coming toward the dining room. My Daddy jumps up from his chair so fast that he knocks it over, just as two policemen enter the room.

My Daddy is on some kind of committee for the town of Oak Bluffs. I don't really understand what it is, but he knows all the policemen. So, when they barge in on our dinner, he calls them by their first names and asks them what they are doing there.

They don't answer him. They just eyeball my brothers and one of them says, "Thomas Culligan?"

My brother Tommy's eyes get wide as he nods and squeaks, "Yes," in a scared little mouse voice.

The policemen move so quickly to Tommy, it is like they didn't even walk there. One minute they are standing in the doorway and the next they are grabbing Tommy by the arms.

"Thomas Culligan," one of them says, his voice booming. "You are under arrest for the rape of a child, please come with us."

The other one went on to tell him stuff about staying quiet and something about a lawyer. It sounds to me like it is a speech that he practiced. I have no idea what he is talking about though, because suddenly there is too much noise. Mommy is screaming. My Daddy is yelling at them to tell him what is going on.

My other three brothers are all trying to talk to Tommy, one louder than the other. The police are wrestling my brother from his chair and putting handcuffs on him, trapping them behind his back. His chair tips over and crashes to the floor, making a loud hollow thump. Someone is crying. Deep, loud cries.

It takes me a minute to realize that the someone is me.

Chapter 7

1982

After Thanksgiving dinner was over and everything was cleaned up, my brothers all left and Mom and I packed up our stuff and headed back to our house.

The next day we took a trip off-Island to go to Boston and stay at Mom's favorite hotel, the Ritz-Carlton. When I was a little girl, my parents went and stayed there once a year for a weekend. They said they liked to go visit their old stomping grounds.

My dad went to medical school there and when they first got married they lived in a small apartment in a building that was called a brownstone. Mom worked at one of the big hospitals as a psychiatric nurse and supported Dad through school. Both of my parents had been raised on the Island - not born there, but they both moved there when they were so young that they didn't remember living anywhere else.

When Dad finished medical school, there was a job offer waiting for him at the MV hospital. He also had several offers in the Boston area. My parents decided if they were going to have children, which of course they were, they were going to move back to the Island. There was no way they wanted to raise kids in the city.

I loved to go off Island; everything was an adventure, even simple things that were most likely not amazing to kids who lived there. Driving on the highway was somewhat scary, but mostly exciting. Tunnels were amazing, overpasses intriguing and stop lights were just plain awesome. We didn't have any of those things at home, and the fastest we ever drove was 40. Going 55 on the highway felt like being on a roller coaster to me. I had a few problems with the inside of buildings.

I loved the outsides, we had nothing on the Island that was over two stories high, so whenever I saw skyscrapers they blew my mind. But elevators, escalators, and revolving doors freaked me right out. If I had the choice, I would always take the stairs. Elevators weren't too bad, and I would go on them if I had to, but I would never, ever go on an escalator.

I think it was because Donny told me that kids got sucked up inside them at the tops and bottoms all the time. The first time I went in a revolving door, I thought it was so cool, but Donny struck again – he got outside and stuck his foot in the door so that I couldn't move it. That was the first and last time I ever used one of those doors.

We got up on Saturday morning and were getting ready to go out for the day, when the phone rang. Mom answered it, listened for a minute and said that it would be fine. She hung up and turned to me.

"That was the front desk. Your father is here."

"Why?" I asked, shocked.

"I don't know. He just showed up. He's on his way up here."

There was a knock on the door and Mom let Dad in.

"What are you doing here?"

Dad chuckled and said, "How could I let my favorite girls come to Boston without me? Besides, I had a reservation for the boat that we made last year. I wasn't going to waste it."

When we were ready to go, we took the subway into the city. Mom liked to go shopping at these stores on Charles Street, which was made of cobblestones. Dad and I waited outside for her.

"Want to do what we did the last time we were here together?" Dad asked.

"I think I'm too old for that now," I said.

Dad laughed and said, "Too old? What about me? I'm older than you!"

"Nah, if it's okay with you, I really don't feel like it."

"Okay. Just remember, you're never too old to have an imagination."

That night we had dinner in the hotel restaurant and my parents discussed the sleeping arrangements for the night.

"How about we do this?" Dad said. "Dora is old enough to stay in a room by herself. I'll get the room and come stay with you."

"No," Mom said. "I'm sticking with what Missy said. I want to make this work and I think we should do what she says."

"Forget Missy. I'm starting to think she got her degree from a Cracker Jack box."

Mom laughed. It was nice to hear her being happy with Dad, but she stuck to her word. Dad got another room and stayed there by himself. I mostly tried to ignore the conversation. I didn't want to think about the fact that my father was so desperate to get laid that he was resorting to practically begging my mother, at the dinner table and in front of his daughter, no less.

I was happy that Mom and Dad seemed to be really enjoying each other's company and I started thinking that if it was going to be like this, maybe it wouldn't be so bad if they got back together. I just really didn't want to think about what my father wanted to do. I also hoped that they wouldn't make the decision until the house was already sold. I never, ever wanted to live there again.

1975

Mommy and Daddy take me on their special trip to Boston. They pretend they want me to come with them, but I think the truth is that they can't find anyone to watch me.

Jim, Pat and Tommy are all old enough to stay home alone, but my mother doesn't think they are old enough to take care of me. Donny is on a Boy Scout camping trip, so they don't have to worry about him.

They take me to see an ice-skating show on our first night there and I love it. I tell Mommy that I want to start taking ice skating lessons so that I can be in a show like that when I grow up. She tells me that the women in the show have been skating since they could walk and I am too old to get started now. She gets into an argument with Daddy over that.

He says my Mommy should be more "encouraging" and stop being such a "pessimist." Mommy says she isn't a "pessimist," she is a "realist". I have no idea what they are talking about, so when we get back to the room I tear a piece of paper from the little notepad in the nightstand. I write "encouraging," "pessimist," and "realist". I plan on looking them up in the dictionary when we get home.

On Saturday we go down to the restaurant and have breakfast and then we take the subway to the stores where Mommy likes to go shopping.

We walk down the cobblestone street and my Daddy tells me all about the history of cobblestones and about how all the streets used to be made of them. My Mommy doesn't really seem to care about the street, just about the shops, so she goes into one and my Daddy and I go with her.

We follow her around the store for a little while, but then we get bored. My Daddy grabs my hand, tells my Mommy we will be outside, and leads me out onto the street.

We find a bench where nobody is sitting and sit down. My Daddy says, "When I was in school and was on my way home, I used to stop and sit here for a while to wind down a little from the day before I went back home to your Mommy. I want to show you what I used to do."

"What did you do?" I ask.

"Just close your eyes and listen," he says.

So, I do and I can hear people walking on the cobblestones. When women with high heels walk by it makes a clip clop sound that echoes through the street. "I hear people's feet," I say.

"Are you sure they're people?" I start to open my eyes but Daddy covers them with his hand. "Keep them closed and keep listening. Don't listen with just your ears."

At first I have no idea what my father means by listening with anything besides my ears, but I trust him, so I keep my eyes closed and try to hear what is going on around me, without thinking about anything else.

"I hear horses!" I exclaim, bouncing up and down on the bench.

"That's right. Hear that one that's near us right now? Who do you think is riding it?"

I listen for a second. "It's a princess!"

"Really?" my father asks. "How do you know that?"

"Because the steps the horse is taking are uneven and that means the horse is being ridden sidesaddle."

"So how do you know it's a princess?"

"Because princesses always ride sidesaddle. They have to because of their gowns. Everyone knows that, silly Daddy."

"That's true, but wait… I hear a clinking sound. What do you suppose that is?"

"I'm not sure. I can't see anything." My eyes are screwed shut tight, but I don't mean with my eyes, and we both know it.

"Me neither," he says. "Wait! Now I see! He's coming around the corner. It's a knight! He's wearing armor. That's the clinking noise. Do you see him?"

And then I do. "His armor is so shiny! I can barely see him because of the sun!"

My Daddy and I sit on that bench for over a half hour, while a medieval parade of Kings, Queens, princes, princesses, knights, jesters, and servants go by us. Oh, the stories we imagine! There are two knights who joust right there in front of us, and a princess who was kidnapped by a group of bandits and thieves is rescued by a handsome prince right at our feet.

"We've got to go," my father says, ripping me from the fantasy world. "Your mother will be wondering where we are for so long."

I open my eyes and am back in Boston in the present. The horses that carried royalty are women in high heels, the horse-drawn carriages are rolling carts in which people lug their work stuff instead of carrying it, or homeless people pushing shopping carts that are filled with everything they own. The knights become the men who walk beside women in high heels, with change jiggling in their pockets, as they hurry to lunch or back to work, or on some type of work-related errand.

My Daddy and I get up, and walking hand-in-hand, head back to the dress store where we left my Mommy 1000 years ago, or a half hour ago, and I look back at the street one more time. I see the women in their heels, walking next to men with change in their pockets, but far away, disappearing around the corner of the cobblestone street, I see something else: the swishing of a horse's tail between the folds of a purple royal gown as it gallops to escape the clutching claws of the fire-breathing dragon.

That night back in the hotel, I am snuggled up in my cot, asleep. I wake up to my parents laughing and whispering but I don't move at all, so they don't know I am awake.

"No, James!" my Mommy whispers loudly, "Dora is right there! She'll wake up."

"Not if we're quiet. Besides, she sleeps like the dead. Come on, it's our vacation."

"You'll just have to wait until it's a vacation that doesn't include our little girl in the same room."

I don't really mean to, but I can't help it, I peek at my parents. My Daddy is laying on top of my Mommy, kissing her all over her face and saying, "Please," and she keeps saying, "No."

I shut my eyes again quickly and roll over, pulling the blankets over my head. This is something that I know about. This is something that happens to me.

The only difference is, my Mommy isn't trying to scream and my Daddy isn't clamping his hand over her mouth.

Chapter 8

1982

When we got back to the house from our trip to Boston, we couldn't have been inside for more than ten minutes when the phone rang. Mom answered it, listened for a minute and then said, "Okay, James, calm down. We'll be right there."

"That was Dad?" I asked. "What's wrong?"

"There's a problem at the house. He wants me to come over right away. You want to take a ride?"

"Sure, I'll come."

When we got to the house the front door was wide open. As we stepped onto the porch, Dad came out of the house dragging Mom's Oriental rug, which was rolled up, behind him.

"What are you doing with that?" Mom asked. "What's wrong with it?"

All Dad said was, "Puke" and he pulled the rug off the porch and threw it onto the grass.

Mom and I went into the house and we gasped at the same time. The first room you could see when you walked in the front door was her sitting room. It was totally trashed. There were red plastic party cups and empty booze bottles all over the floor and the furniture. Ashtrays overflowed all over Mom's coffee table and end tables, and obviously when they got full people just started putting their cigarettes out on the table and on the floor.

There were little burn marks everywhere. There were garbage bags full of cups and booze bottles and an empty garbage bag box, as though someone had started cleaning up but ran out of bags before they could finish. We were just standing there staring when Dad came back in the house.

"Donny has pushed it way too far this time. I can't believe I couldn't go away for one night and trust him," he said.

I heard a car pull up in the driveway and went over to the door. It was Jim's car, he was driving and Donny was in the passenger seat. They got out and Donny grabbed a bag out of the trunk. I could see a box of garbage bags sticking out of the top.

"He's back," I said.

Dad rushed past me and out onto the porch. "What the hell happened in here, Donny?"

"I...I..." Donny stammered.

"I'm done," my father said. "It's time you packed your stuff and found a new place to live."

"James..." Mom began.

"No," Dad interrupted. "He can go rent an apartment off Island, near school. I don't need this right now. You're barely even old enough to drink and I know most of your friends aren't old enough! What did you have? A bunch of under-aged kids here, drinking in my house? I'm a town selectman, Donny. Did you stop to think how this could have affected me? What if somebody left and had an accident? Not to mention the house is destroyed!"

"Dad," Jim said. "It's not his fault. He didn't even have the party. I did. My apartment is too small, so I figured I would just have one over here and it got a little out of hand. I had every intention of cleaning and fixing everything up before you got home. I'm sorry. And there was nobody here under-age drinking. I didn't even let Donny stay around. I'll make everything right, okay, Dad? And I swear it will never happen again."

Of course, my father was still pissed at Jim, but what could he have done? Donny was the only one who had anything to lose, so Jim took the fall. I was amazed at how naïve my parents actually were.

When we were kids my brothers had this thing they called "The Parent Pact". It meant that no matter what, they would never tell on each other and they would cover whenever it helped. They might as well have called it "The Brother Pact," because for most of my childhood I wasn't included in it. I tattled on them whenever I could, and they did everything they could to get me in trouble.

One day though, it all changed and my brothers decided to protect me for once. It had to do with a guinea pig named Piggily-Wiggily.

1975

Tommy gets Piggily-Wiggily for his birthday from Uncle Les. He is a guinea pig. His daughter got one from the pet store and it had babies. Tommy wants one so bad and begs Mommy and Daddy to let him get one. They say no, but then on his birthday Piggily-Wiggily is there, in a cage with a big bow on top. Tommy is so excited. He snuggles him and kisses him, sets up the cage in his room, gives him his toys, and then forgets all about him.

He never takes him out of the cage and doesn't let anyone else either. I beg him to let me hold him, but he never lets me.

One day none of my brothers are home and Mommy is busy making dinner, so I sneak into Tommy's room. I go over to the cage and peek in at Piggily-Wiggily. He looks up at me and squeaks. I decide I am just going to hold him for a second and Tommy will never even know.

Unfortunately for me, I don't realize that because nobody ever holds Piggily-Wiggily, he isn't the cute, cuddly little guy that he appears to be. He is scared to death of people. As soon as I get my hands on him and lift him from the cage he starts squealing like crazy and squirming around. He bites my finger. I drop him to the floor, and then he bites my toe. I kick him as hard as I can. I don't mean to hurt him, I just want him to stop biting me. But I watch as he tumbles over three times and then lays totally still in the middle of Tommy's rug.

As I stand there, willing him with my eyes to just move, Tommy's door opens and he comes in. Tommy looks at me, and then his eyes go to the guinea pig, who is still in the same position. "Dora, what's going on here?" he asks through gritted teeth.

"I'm sorry, I didn't mean to do it! He was biting me real hard and I dropped him, and then I accidently kicked him. Look!"

I hold up my foot to show him where Piggily-Wiggily sank his teeth into my toe; where I expect to see blood gushing, and I am a little bit surprised and upset by the fact that I can't even see the teeth marks. Tommy goes to where Piggily-Wiggily's body is and picks him up gently. He carries him to the cage and puts him back inside. The door opens again and Jim, Pat, and Donny come barging in.

"What's up?" Jim asks, jutting his chin toward me. "What's she doing in here?"

"I was just about to ask her that," Tommy replies. "So, Dora, what are you doing in here?"

"I just wanted to hold him. Just for a minute. You never do, Tommy, and I thought he was lonely."

My brothers all glance at Piggily-Wiggily, who still has not moved in his cage. "What happened?" Jim asks.

I start to cry, hoping this will make them feel bad for me and repeat the story.

"Oh, this is bad, Dora. Do you know how bad this is? You murdered him. If Mom and Dad find out…" Jim says.

"I know," I say, sobbing.

"Well, I think I have an idea. Have a seat everyone." Big brother to the rescue.

All of my brothers sit, on the bed, on Tommy's chair. I sit on the floor as far away from Piggily-Wiggily's body as I can get. Jim opens the door wide and checks the hallway, to make sure Mommy isn't coming, then he goes over to Piggily-Wiggily's cage and lifts him out.

"Well, he is definitely dead, but there is no obvious trauma, so I think we can make this work."

"What are you talking about, Jim?" Pat asks.

"We're gonna have to tell Mom and Dad that he's dead. It may take them a while to notice, but they will eventually, so we are going to have to come up with a story and stick to it."

"What are we supposed to tell them?" Tommy asks, upset. "I'm not taking the blame for this!"

"No, Dora is going to have to take the blame, but we can just make it out like it was more of...an accident..."

"It was an accident!" I yell.

"Shh. It was, and wasn't, Dora. You did kick him, and you will get in trouble for that, even if you didn't mean to hurt him."

"Kill him!" Tommy hollers, jumping to his feet. "Why don't you say it like it is? She killed him!"

"Right, but that part was an accident," Jim says. "So, here's how it will go down. We'll tell Mom and Dad that Piggily-Wiggily accidently got left in the chair, and Dora sat on him. Okay? Can we all agree to that?"

"What, so I get blamed for leaving him in a chair?" Tommy asks, plopping back in his chair.

"Isn't that better than the truth? For both you and her? I mean you do totally neglect the thing. If you held it once in a while, it wouldn't have freaked when Dora tried to hold it. You're as much to blame as she is for his murder."

So that's the story we tell. We have a funeral and bury Piggily-Wiggily in a shoe box in the backyard. Mommy and Daddy didn't question how Piggily-Wiggily came to be in a chair or how I happened to come along and not notice him before I sat. His cage gets stored in the garage and nobody talks about him again.

The next day Tommy comes into my room carrying a bumpy thing that is wrapped messily in leftover Christmas paper. "Sit down, Dora. We need to talk," he says.

I sit on my bed and look at the present, "What's that?"

"It's for you, but you need to listen to me first, okay? We did 'rock, paper, scissors, shoot' and I was the one who had to come talk to you. We want to let you in on "The Parent Pact". Do you know what that means?" Tommy asks.

"We'll never, ever tell on each other?"

"That's right. No matter what. After Piggily-Wiggily, we decided that it was time to let you in. So, you can promise?"

"I promise," I exclaim, barely able to stay sitting.

"Okay. We all chipped in and bought this for you and by taking it, you swear to the rules of "The Parent Pact". So, you can?"

"Uh huh," I reach for the present.

He pulls the present out of my reach. "You understand that if you don't, we'll have to tell Mom and Dad about Piggily-Wiggily?"

"Yes, Tommy, okay. Can I have it now?" He hands me the package and I rip off the paper. It is a stuffed guinea pig and it looks just like Piggily-Wiggily. I squeeze it to my chest. "I love him. I'm going to name him Piggily-Wiggily!"

"Good," Tommy says. "That will help you to remember."

Chapter 9

1982

Mom and I stayed and helped Dad, Jim, and Donny clean the house. Jim and Donny opened the box of garbage bags and cleaned up the trash. Mom had me get some furniture polish from the cabinet and we tried to buff the cigarette burns from the tables. A couple of them did buff out because they were only stains and not actual burns, but some of them didn't come out, no matter how hard we rubbed them.

Mom had me go out to the garage to get a pile of newspapers and then we wrapped up the lamps and the glass inserts from the tables so that Mom could take the tables to the refinisher. After we lugged the tables outside and stored the lamps and the glass inserts in the closet, Mom inspected the couch and the loveseat for burn holes.

Mom sent me upstairs to go look in her bureau for the business card of a man who did furniture refinishing in Vineyard Haven. I went up the stairs and walking down the hall I noticed that my father's door was shut, which was strange.

When Mom and I lived there, the door was always open during the day. I put my hand on the knob and turned it quickly. The only reason why I didn't scream was because I clamped my hand over my mouth or I would have. There was a half-naked girl laying on the end of my mother's bed pulling on her thong. She was obviously trying to get dressed in a hurry because her shirt was on inside out and backwards.

"Who are you?" I asked.

"My name is Nikki."

"I didn't ask you what your name was, I asked you who you are. What are you doing in my parents' bedroom?"

"I was here, with, um, a guy, um, there was a party, see, and he told me to wait here, that he would be right back…"

Something on top of my mother's bureau caught my eye. I closed my parents' bedroom door and walked over to the bureau where I saw Donny's license laying in a pile of white powder and next to a rolled-up dollar bill. I wasn't totally clueless about stuff, but it did take me a minute to realize it was cocaine, or maybe even heroin.

"That guy, was his name Donny?"

"Yeah, that's it! He said this was his house. He told me that his parents had died in a plane crash and left it to him in their will."

"Well, that was a lie. And his parents are right downstairs and probably about to come up here any minute, so I would suggest that while I clean this mess up over here you get those sheets off the bed."

I unrolled the dollar and took it and Donny's license into the bathroom where I rinsed them off in the sink. I got some toilet paper, wet it down and went back into the bedroom and wiped the top of the bureau.

The girl had finished getting dressed and was just starting to try to take the sheets off the bed, so I went back into the bathroom to find a set that Dad probably wouldn't notice were different from the ones she was taking off. She still didn't even have everything off, so I told her that she could just forget it.

I would make the bed myself. It was pretty clear she only knew how to dirty sheets, not clean up after herself. I told her she needed to follow me and be quiet. I was going to show her how she could get out.

I led her to the attic stairs and letting her go first, we climbed up. I told her she needed to climb out the window, and closing it behind her, she should go over the peak of the roof and there she would see a trellis she could climb down and make her way safely to the ground. Then she could go through the woods and head into town to go back to wherever she needed to go. I didn't bother to ask her if she wanted to leave a message, like that she would call him or something, because I assumed that since she didn't even know his name, there wasn't any long-standing relationship there.

I stayed at the top of the attic stairs watching until she crawled over the peak of the roof and I couldn't see her anymore. I went back to my parent's room and hurried to remake the bed before my mother decided to come up herself looking for the business card. As I put the sheets on the bed, I thought about "The Parent Pact".

1975

After I become a part of "The Parent Pact" I feel really special, not because I think I am going to get away with anything, but because I feel grown up. It was like before my brothers thought I was a little kid and now they think I am big enough to be with them in their club. I still didn't totally trust them though.

I have a feeling that if they can tell on me to stop themselves from getting in trouble, they will. I start to set up little tests to see what they will do.

One day when Mommy is outside working in her garden, I get a popsicle from the freezer and go into her sitting room to eat it. I sit on the love seat and open it up, sticking my hands under the plastic and shoving the wrapper in between the cushions.

Donny walks by just as I take my first bite. "What are you doing?"

"Nothing."

"You better get outta there with that popsicle before..." He stops talking.

"Before what?" I ask, taking another popsicle bite.

"Before Mom comes in and catches you."

I jump up from the seat and walk past Donny, smiling at him as I did. Test number one - passed.

Later that day when my mother comes back inside she tells my brothers to keep on watching me and she goes into her sitting room to relax for a little while before she has to start dinner. I wait in my bedroom, but I keep my door open so I can hear everything. It only takes a couple of minutes and then I hear her yell my name. I run halfway down the stairs and stop when I see her standing in the doorway with the popsicle wrapper in her hand, "Dora, what is this?"

"A wrapper?" I ask.

All of my brothers come around the corner from the TV room and stand there watching us.

"Are you trying to say it's not yours? Who else would have been eating a popsicle in my room and would stuff the wrapper in between the cushions? Do you expect me to believe one of your brothers did it? Jim, Tommy, Pat, Donny, is this yours?"

I look at Donny as he leans against the wall and crosses his arms in front of his chest. He turns his head away from my mother, looking back into the TV room. Everyone else looks at me.

I look down at my feet. My voice barely comes out in a whisper, "It's mine."

"Why in God's name would you do that? Wrappers go in the garbage can, Dora! You know that!"

"I'm sorry. I didn't mean to."

"Well, you march down here right this minute, young lady, and go throw this in the garbage can. Then you can stay in your room until I call you for dinner."

I walk down the stairs and when I get to the bottom, Donny looks up at me. I wink at him, well kind of blink, because I can't really do it. He turns and walks back into the living room where I can hear him laughing. Test number two - passed.

After I throw the wrapper away, I go up to my room; like usual, I don't mind getting sent to my room. I had just gotten my dictionary back and had a bunch of words to look up. Over the next couple of weeks, I set up more tests for my brothers and they pass all of them. What I hadn't realized at first is that they were setting up tests for me also.

One day, my mother, Donny, and I go to the grocery store. Donny has money with him but he is twenty-three cents short to buy a bag of chips he wants. He begs my mother to lend him some money, promising he will pay her back as soon as we get home.

My mother gives him a quarter and when we get home, she goes into her sitting room, and leaves her purse on the kitchen table. Donny sits down near her purse and waits until it is quiet, until our mother finishes setting up her room divider and has to be sitting down. Then he reaches into her change purse and takes out a quarter.

He looks at me, right into my eyes, but he talks to our mother, "I have the quarter for you, to pay you back."

He gets up and goes to her room to give her the quarter. I hear her laugh, "I have to tell you, Donny, I didn't believe you really had the money to pay me back. I'm glad you are being honest."

"I wouldn't have told you I had it, if I didn't."

Donny comes back into the kitchen, and as he heads out the other door and into the dining room, he winks at me.

Chapter 10

1982

Olivia was not the only person from my childhood who I reconnected with when I joined the jock group. There was a boy named Jared who I had a wicked crush on from first grade through sixth grade. He was a year older than me, so by the time I moved up to sixth grade, he was gone to junior high.

By the time I started junior high, I kinda just forgot about him. He was my first real boy kiss, behind the tree on our elementary school playground.

Similar to most high school romances, mine and Jared's did not begin with us talking to each other at all. It began in the cafeteria with Olivia and some other girls from the basketball team.

"Jared thinks you're cute," Olivia said.

"Really?" I asked.

"Uh-huh"a girl named Sally said. "He likes you. A lot."

"That's cool," I said. "I've had a crush on him since first grade."

Everybody at the table started cracking up.

"What's so funny?"

"He said the exact same thing!" Olivia said.

After that day Jared started hanging around with us. He and like two or three of his friends started eating lunch at our table. He also waited for me to get out of basketball; because the boys' team started their practice earlier than us, they got done earlier.

He walked me to the locker room, waited for me to get ready, walked me to the bus, and sat with me. We weren't on the regular bus together, but we were on the same late bus. Whenever we had away games, the boys and girls' teams shared a bus and he would sit with me then, too.

On one of our away game bus trips, he got up quickly when we pulled into the school parking lot where our games were. He leaned over and gave me a quick kiss on the lips.

"Good luck," he said, and hurried to the front of the bus so he would be the first one off. I was the last. I sat there with my hand on my lips, the heat of his searing my skin.

Both the boys' and girls' teams won that day and I scored the winning basket for my team, so I was famous, at my school, for one day anyway.

My family, or more specifically, my brothers, went bananas. They were so thrilled that I was finally going to join their ranks, and possibly get dubbed MVP of our high school basketball team, as they had all done at one time or another. Basketball, and sports in general, were held in high esteem in my family.

So far I have been a disappointment to everyone, and it was because of Stacy.

1980

My career as an athlete is ruined before it even begins, and it is all because I met Stacy. I met her on the first day of junior high; her family just moved to the Island over the summer. We have an assembly in the auditorium and are assigned seats alphabetically. Her last name is Cullen, so we sit next to each other.

It is pretty obvious right from the start that Stacy has no respect for school or authority. She talks during the whole assembly, mimicking the principal and making commentaries on the rules of the school. She has all of us sitting near her practically wetting our pants from laughing so hard. And none of the teachers or the principal ever catch us. Stacy seems to be impervious to the attention of authority.

At lunchtime she calls me over to sit with her, Brandy and Laurie. I look all around the cafeteria and don't see anyone else I really want to eat lunch with, so I sit with them.

I have known Brandy and Laurie pretty much my whole life, but I wasn't ever friends with them. I go to the Vineyard Haven Co-Op Preschool with Laurie. My father built the sandbox there and Laurie gets a fat-lip when she trips and falls out. She says that my father is stupid and built a crummy sandbox. She is lucky she already had a fat lip, or I would have given her one.

When we start regular school, she makes friends with Brandy, so I never really bother with her either. I find Stacy amusing, but I'm sure I want to be friends with her. Brandy and Laurie attach themselves to her on the first day of seventh grade, as though they had been waiting their entire school careers for someone to come along and be their leader.

I learn pretty quickly though, with Stacy, it doesn't really matter what anyone else wants, if she wants to be friends with you, it is gonna happen.

I am really excited about starting junior high because of the sports teams. Elementary school doesn't have any real teams. When I was little I was on the swim team in Vineyard Haven at the Mansion, but after I quit swimming I didn't join anything else. The day we get announcements for fall soccer, I make it to the cafeteria before Stacy, Brandy, and Laurie and am sitting there just picking at my lunch and reading over the form. When Stacy gets there, she sits across from me and snatches the paper from my hands.

"What'cha reading, Culligan?" she asks.

"Nothing. Paperwork for soccer tryouts. Give it back."

Stacy pretends to study it for a minute and then flips it over her shoulder. Within seconds it is trampled by passing students. It is torn and disappears under their feet.

"Whoops, sorry."

"Stacy," I groan and get up to retrieve the paper from the floor but it is ruined. "What did you do that for?"

"You weren't really thinking about doing it, were you?"

"Yeah, maybe I was. So what?"

"It's your funeral, Culligan. If you want to go and get all dirty and smelly running around a muddy field with a bunch of lesbos, go for it."

Brandy and Laurie come to the table and sit down. "Go for what?" Laurie asks.

"Turning herself into a social outcast, that's all. Culligan here was going to try out for soccer."

"That's lame," Brandy says. "Why would you want to go and do something like that?"

"I don't know. I just thought…."

"Well quit thinking about it. Thank god you met me so I can keep you in line. You'd be ostracized in a week without me!"

They all laugh, and I laugh along with them. Deep down, though, I have a gnawing thought: who will I be outcast from? Them? All three of them? I plan to go to the office at the end of day and ask for another soccer form, but then I never do.

Instead, I do what they wanted me to do and don't try out. When it comes time for basketball tryouts, I know I will never get away with not trying out. My brothers will freak out.

I bring the forms home, making sure Stacy didn't see them, and have Mom fill them out. My brothers are so excited. They give me pep-talks and tell me how junior high basketball will set the precedence for my high school basketball career. Every night before try-outs, at least one of them practices with me.

The night before try-outs, they all go with me to the Oak Bluffs basketball courts and we practice for hours. They make me run drills and practice shooting while they play defense. I am so exhausted by the time we get home I am glad I'm not actually trying out for the team.

The next day after school, I go to Stacy's house. She has a magazine with a cool hairstyle and wants to try it with my hair. She spends like an hour curling it and pinning it up with bobby pins. I have to admit it looked pretty good. It is a shame I am going to ruin it.

I leave her house and go back to school. I wait around until all the girls who had tried out for the team left the locker room, then I rush in and take the bobby pins out of my hair. I wet my hair down in the shower and dry it with my shorts and t-shirt, so that they will be damp, too. Then I wait outside for Mom to pick me up.

I am pretty sure nobody will believe that I don't make the first cut for the team, so I have to keep up the charade for the next day. I tell my brothers I made first cut, and they drag me back to the courts to practice again.

I do the same thing after school the next day. I go to Stacy's house and then go back to the school, in time to meet Mom and looking like I just had a try-out. I tell them I made the second cut.

The next day I go home looking all depressed, which isn't even actually that hard. I did want to play basketball, I had been conditioned for it since I was a little kid. Plus, I was lying to my family, and it didn't feel good.

"You're kidding!" Jim exclaims when I tell them at dinner that I got cut from the team. "How could you have gotten cut? You're better than Donny for cripes sakes!"

"Watch your mouth, Jim," Mom says.

"Shut up, Jim! She is not!"

"I said cripes, Mom. And yeah, she is, Donny. I just can't believe it. I'm going to go down there after school tomorrow and talk to the coach. It's still that Mrs. Newton, right?"

"No, Jim, don't. Please don't talk to her, just let it go," I say.

"It's only junior high," Dad says. "She'll practice a little harder, and she can try out next year. A lot of people who go on to be great on their high school teams didn't play in junior high."

My brothers make me practice with them every day that school year. In the summer, Jim gets a job with Oak Bluffs Rec and runs a basketball clinic. He makes me come to everyone and then practice at night, too.

By the time eighth grade basketball tryouts come around, I am too good to pretend I got cut, so I have to fake an injury. Dad confirms I am injured and I hobble around on crutches for a couple of months. Jim, Pat, and Donny all act like it is the end of the world that I can't go out for basketball. I'm not so sure about Dad.

As a trained doctor, it seems like a fake injury would be obvious to him, but he diagnoses me with some fancy medical condition and says I can't put any pressure on my leg.

After basketball is over for the year, he declares me cured and sends me on my way to be tortured by my brothers with extra basketball practice to make up for the time I missed.

Chapter 11

1982

The same night of the away game where I scored the winning basket, Jared called me at home and asked me out on a date to Papa John's. When I told Mom, she was so excited she put on "Walking on Sunshine" and started dragging me all over the house dancing.

"Mom, stop!" I said laughing as the song ended. "It's not the prom! We're going out for pizza."

"Dora, it doesn't matter where you're going! It's your first date!"

"Mom, I've been on hundreds of dates. This is just the only one you've heard about because it's the first one I'm not getting paid for." She cocked her eyebrow at me.

"Kidding!"

Mom looked at her watch, "You're going to need a new outfit."

"I have tons of homework."

"Tomorrow, then? When is your date?"

"Saturday night."

"That's even better. We can go Saturday morning and I'll call Carolyn and make a hair appointment for the afternoon."

"Whatever, Mom," I said as I walked to my room to start my homework.

My poor mother, having to live her life through me. Too bad it wasn't more exciting.

By noon time on Saturday I was pretty sure I wouldn't make it to my date because I would be dead of embarrassment. We were standing in front of Lillian's of the Vineyard before it even opened at nine o'clock. When they opened the door to let us in, Mom went in before me and held the door.

When I walked in she made out like it was a grand entrance or something, "Ladies, may I have your attention! My lovely daughter, Dora, is going on her first date with a real boy tonight! She needs a smashing dress!"

"That's right, Mom," I said quietly as I walked by her. "My first date with a real boy. Should we mention the date I went on with Pinocchio?"

For the next three hours I was measured, poked, prodded, examined, and talked about as though I wasn't right there, while they tried to find the perfect dress to "accentuate my features." Lillian's had nothing I liked, so after two more stores, two more grand entrances, and a ton of sales ladies feeling up my boobs and my hips, I settled on a dress that I didn't really like, but they all did, so I took it just so we didn't have to go to another store.

For the $50 my mother paid for the dress, I got a bunch of free advice from the sales ladies.

"When he compliments you on your dress, say, 'Oh, this old thing?'"

"Flip your hair back with your hand, like this," (free demonstration).

"You have beautiful shoulders, you want to make sure he sees them."

As far as I knew, guys were into boobs and behinds, I wasn't sure how shoulders fit into the equation.

"Eat before you go out. Then just order a small salad, but don't eat it all."

"And for heaven's sake, don't ask for a doggie bag!"

By the time we got to the hairdresser, I thought my head might have been spinning around too fast for her to do anything with my hair. Of course, as soon as we stepped in the door, Mom made her announcement about me going on my first date. It was even worse than the clothing stores. Not only did I have all the hairdressers giving me advice, but the ladies who were getting their hair done pitched in their two cents as well.

There was one guy there and he told me, "Order dinner and eat it. There's nothing us guys hate more than a date who orders a salad and then doesn't even finish it. We're taking you out to eat, so eat!"

Then Carolyn styled my hair so it swooped down and curled in front of my shoulders, hiding them. All of the advice I had been getting was just a little too contradictory, so I decided to forget it all and just go with what felt right to me.

Jared only had his driver's permit and didn't want his mother chauffeuring our date, so we just met at the restaurant. When Mom and I pulled up, he was already sitting there in his mom's car. He rushed over and opened my door for me and took my hand to help me out.

"Hi, Mrs. Culligan," he said to Mom. To me he said, "Wow, you look beautiful."

When we were waiting in line to place our order, he said, "That is an amazing dress, Adorable."

I didn't even have time to think about if I should say, "This old thing?" or if I should tell him how my mother dragged me all over town to find it, because suddenly I was mortified.

Of course, he knew my real name! We had gone to school together since I was in kindergarten, "Oh, God, Jared, don't call me that. I've worked really hard to keep that name secret."

He laughed and said, "Why? It's a beautiful name. And it suits you. You're a beautiful girl."

"Thanks for saying I'm beautiful, but Adorable is an idiotic name and you know it. In fact, I'm considering suing my parents."

We ordered our pizza, then got our drinks and sat down to wait for them to call our number.

"So, Dora, so what's been going on in your life? I don't think we've had a real conversation since sixth grade."

"Not much. How about you?"

"Same old. Same old. Watching you from afar and wishing I could ask you out."

"Wishing you could? Why couldn't you?"

"Would you have said yes?" he asked.

"I did, didn't I?"

"I meant before," he clarified, and took a bite of his pizza.

"I probably would have," I conceded, shrugging..

"Yeah? Well I couldn't have asked you anyway."

"How come?" I asked.

"That Stacy bitch would have never let me close enough to you to ask you out."

"Did people think we were…?" I asked, suddenly mortified.

"Oh no, that's not what I meant. I just meant she wouldn't have thought I was good enough for one of her little followers."

"I would think it would've been the other way around. Mr. Cool Jock, Most Valuable Player of the Varsity basketball team."

"Nah, we would never be cooler than you." He did a fake southern drawl, "The meanest girls this side of the Mississippi."

"Hmm. You probably don't even know the extent of it."

1981

By the time we start eighth grade Stacy is the queen bee of the school that she imagined herself to be in seventh, and by association, Brandy, Laurie, and I are, too.

When we walk down the hall, we don't do it single file like you are supposed to. We walk in a line that stretches across the entire hallway, and people move out of the way to let us go by. Nobody dares to sit in our seats in the cafeteria, even when we aren't there. Our school has two separate shifts for lunch and we have second lunch. During first lunch, our table stays empty.

People are definitely afraid of Stacy. I think even the teachers are. She hardly goes to class and when she does make it, she screws off the whole period, yet she never gets in trouble.

Stacy has what we all call a "victim of the week". She finds one person who somehow doesn't meet her standards and harasses them until she gets bored and moves on to someone else. I don't actually ever say anything to her victims, but I guess I am just as guilty as she is. I stand behind her and laugh at whatever she says. I think I am always just glad that I am not on the other side.

The year before, being in seventh grade, Stacy couldn't really do things like this, but as an eighth grader, and the oldest in the school, she is able to do it. Her first victim is actually in eighth grade, too. Her name is Annabelle and the year before she had the most beautiful long hair.

When we came back from summer vacation it was all chopped off as short as a boy's. I wasn't sure if Stacy actually found out, or if she just guessed, but she ran around telling everyone, "You know why Annabelle got all her hair cut off? She had lice and that was the only way they could get rid of it."

"Shut up, Stacy!" Annabelle says to her, but she doesn't deny it isn't true. Stacy tells everyone and even writes it on the bathroom stall.

After a couple days of that rumor, Annabelle starts ignoring Stacy, so Stacy comes up with a new rumor.

"Annabelle's scheduled for a sex change and her boy name is going to be Andrew. She is just trying out the hairstyle to make sure that she likes it before going ahead with the surgery."

I feel pretty bad for the seventh graders who are Stacy's victims. Here they are, new to junior high, and they not only had to get used to a new building, new teachers, and switching classes for the first time, but they also had to contend with being picked on by Stacy. At least she had a short attention span, and nobody had to put up with her for long.

Sometimes I picture myself getting in between Stacy and whoever her victim is and saying that it is enough, and that Stacy should just leave the person alone. I never do it, though. I just stand behind her and laugh, but I feel sick to my stomach every time. This is not who I was, but for some reason I go along with it.

Seventh graders seem to be really little and I think eighth graders forget that they used to be little, too. There is a girl named Devin who is really small, even for a seventh grader.

I am usually not sure how Stacy comes up with her rumors, but she starts a crazy one about Devin, based on our history class. We are learning about orphan trains and indentured servitude.

She tells everyone who will listen to her, "The reason why Devin is so small is because she is really only ten. Her parents bought her as an indentured servant when she was six, but the guys who sold her said that she was eight, because they didn't have a birth certificate for her and had to give them a fake one."

I am absolutely disgusted with Stacy for starting the rumor, but of course I do nothing about it. Devin is really traumatized by Stacy's rumor and spends a lot of time crying. Then she is absent for three days in a row. That is actually a good thing for her, because by then, Stacy is on to somebody else.

The bad thing is, that somebody else is me.

Mom gives me long johns that are passed down through all my brothers but are still in good condition. I don't think it is a big deal, it's not like they are underwear or something. One day I wear them to school and our teacher asks me to get something for her off the top shelf.

When I stretch up onto my tippytoes, my shirt goes up and my pants go down a little. Stacy sees the top part of the long johns, with the tell-tale blue and red boy's underwear stripe, and starts telling everyone that I am wearing boy's underwear.

"Stacy, they are not underwear," I tell her. "They're long johns. Big difference."

She doesn't care. When I get to school the next day, people look at me strangely and laugh when I walk past them. It takes me all day, but I find out what new twist she put on the rumor: she tells everyone, "Dora confessed to me that she's fucking her brother. She told me that they had to quickly get dressed so their mother wouldn't catch them, and they accidently switched underwear."

Since we are friends, people believe the rumor. I am an outcast for more than a week.

When Stacy starts picking on someone else, I wish I could say I did what I always dreamed of doing. I wish I stood between Stacy and whoever she was bullying and said in my loudest voice, "Stacy! Leave her alone!"

But I can't. I do, however, not stand behind Stacy and laugh when she picks on someone anymore. I walk away. Brandy and Laurie notice, but Stacy never does, and they don't tell her. I guess at that point they realize that nobody, not even they, are safe from Stacy and her rumors.

Chapter 12

1982

Mom and Dad continued going to their marriage counselor and go on dates. I was really happy for Mom, she seemed happier than she ever was. In fact, whenever she got around Dad she got all silly and giggly. I would say she acted like a high school girl in love, but even I didn't act like that with Jared. She still wasn't sleeping with him, and she told me that they were "getting to know each other again". I guessed that made sense. Maybe Missy wasn't such a crackpot after all.

I was sort of having the same dilemma myself. I really liked Jared, was even starting to fall in love with him. All we had done was made out and he felt my tits up a couple of times. I was starting to think that I wanted to do more, but something was holding me back. I think I was afraid.

I suppose that made sense, too, since I had never done anything more than kiss one guy (and Jared was that guy) but it still felt like it was more than just that. I was lucky, though, because Jared didn't try to push anything on me. In fact, it was me who initiated our first kiss. I thought that if I hadn't, we never would have even done that.

On Christmas Eve, Mom and I went and slept at the house. She had me sleep in the big room again. Even though I was afraid to go in, I fortunately didn't have any memories. I took my clothes out of my bag and put them away in the drawer.

I grabbed my toothbrush and toothpaste and headed for the bathroom. Donny used this one and it was absolutely disgusting. I grabbed the sponge and cleaner out of the cabinet and scrubbed the sink and the toilet. I rinsed everything down and turned toward the shower. I knew I was going to have to clean it, too. After touching Donny's nastiness in the sink and the toilet, I was going to have to take a shower.

The shower curtain was all bunched up and halfway falling off the rod. I told myself that I should just go ask Dad if I could use the shower in his room, but in the end I knew I wouldn't. I was afraid of more than the grossness I knew I was behind the curtain. I was afraid of the memory that I knew was waiting for me.

1976

For a month or so after the funeral, with my brothers hounding me all the time, I never have any time alone to think. Finally, I get an idea on how I can get a few minutes to myself. I tell them I am going upstairs for a bath and for the first time since Tommy died, nobody comes with me.

Every other time when I take a bath one of them comes upstairs with me and follows me around while I get my pajamas from my room and my towel from the linen closet. Whichever brother it was would go into the bathroom and fill the tub. Just before I got undressed my brother would leave and shut the door, but he would sit outside the bathroom and talk to me the whole time I was in the bathroom.

That night I pick bath-time to be right after the first commercial of Happy Days because I figure nobody will follow me. I am right.

The first thing I think about is a lady at the funeral who was dressed almost as stupidly as I was. She had been talking to another lady and she said, "What a shame. He had so much potential. Why these kids do this kind of stuff, I'll never understand."

"Didn't you hear about him?" the other lady had asked.

"Hear what?"

"He molested a little girl. They were looking to put him away for twenty years."

"I didn't hear anything!" she said. "My husband and I just got back from Florida. We spend the winter there. How horrible! I don't know them very well. My husband works with the father. They always seemed like a nice family."

"You just never know, huh?"

I hear other people talking about some kind of note. A man asks, "Does anyone know if he left a note?"

A woman replies, "I heard he did. I heard that he admitted to molesting that girl and said he was too guilty to go on living, knowing how much he hurt her and her family."

"That's not the worst of it!" another woman says. "He confessed to molesting his own sister!" I have no idea what molesting means and I plan on going upstairs after everyone leaves and looking it up in the dictionary. I have the two other words I needed to look up, also.

Since I don't even really know how my brother died, I am also pretty confused about what they mean by "too guilty to go on living". It doesn't take long for me to find another group to fill in the blanks for me.

"I feel so bad for his mother," a woman says. "First to have to face the fact that your own child is a molester, but then to have to deal with him killing himself!"

"And so violently, too!" another woman says. "I heard his older brother had a hunting gun and he took it, went out on the roof of the house. Put the gun under his chin and…"

As I sit in the bathtub and think about the conversations, something just doesn't seem right, but I can't figure out what it is. It seems to me like there was something else. Something that…

"Dora! Are you in the tub?" Jim yells from the other side of the door.

"Yeah. I'm in here," I yell back.

"What are you doing? You know we don't like you to be up here alone! What if you drowned?"

"I'm not gonna drown, Jim!"

"You've been in there long enough. Let the water out and get dressed," he says.

"I haven't even washed my hair yet," I complain.

"Okay, hurry up and do it. There's a movie on I want to see."

"Go watch it," I answer. "I'm fine."

I hear the scrape of the chair as he pulls it in front of the door.

"No, it's okay. Go ahead, wash your hair and tell me what you learned in school today."

Chapter 13

1982

Christmas morning was nothing like when we were kids. Donny and I used to wake up before it was even light and raid our stockings. Then we would go into Mom's sitting room (making sure we got all of the chocolate off our hands first) and we would dig through the pile of presents and shake ours, trying to guess what was inside.

One year, Donny brought a roll of tape down with him. We opened the ends of all our presents, saw what they were and then taped them back up. That pretty much ruined Christmas for us. We had to pretend we were surprised by what we got. We were allowed to wake our parents up at 7 o'clock. Dad, always the jokester, would act like he was so tired and couldn't get out of bed, even though on workdays he was out of the house before 7.

He would say, "I just need a few more minutes. Come back at 8."

Donny and I would be so excited and we would jump on the bed till he got up. He would stumble downstairs, start to walk into the sitting room, and then turn around and go into the kitchen.

"What are you doing, Daddy?" Donny and I would cry out.

"Coffee..." he would say. "I need coffee, first."

Donny and I would sit with him and try to get him to hurry. When he finally finished, he would get up, yawn and stretch and say, "I'm going to get dressed now."

"No, Daddy! Presents!"

"Your mother didn't tell you? This year we're going to church first."

Of course, we didn't actually go to church before we opened our presents, but I swear Dad got us with that same line every year.

Christmas had been progressively losing its magic as I got older and now that I was in high school, it wasn't a big deal at all. Mom actually had to come and wake me up. She threw open my door and called, "Good morning, Sunshine!"

"Ugg," I groaned. "Can you give me until 8?"

"I would, except it's already 10 o'clock. Come on. Get up, Christmas girl. Jim is already here and he's not going to be for long. He's driving out to Maria's family's for dinner."

I sat up and rubbed my eyes. "You're letting him?"

"He's twenty-four, Dora. I don't 'let' him do anything. He does what he wants," Mom said.

"Are you mad at him?" I asked.

"I'm disappointed," she said. "But there's nothing I can do about it. Are you getting up, or what?"

"Nope." I grabbed her arm and pulled her onto the bed. "You stay here and snuggle with me. Let Jim leave and go to stupid Maria's house."

"My mother used to say, 'A son is a son till he takes a wife, a daughter's a daughter all of her life.' I think I'm starting to understand what she meant."

"Uh huh. I am yours forever and ever," I said.

We didn't stay in my bed and snuggle though. Mom made me get out of bed and go downstairs when Jim started yelling up that he was going to have to leave soon.

When we got into the sitting room, Jim came over and hugged me. "Merry Christmas, Sis." I cringed when he touched me. I didn't mean to, it just happened automatically, but I was pretty sure he didn't notice.

"Merry Christmas, Jim."

"Jeepers," Dad said. "What took you two so long? I sent you to bring Dora down, Rainy and I thought I was going to have to send a search party to look for both of you!"

Mom laughed, or giggled, I should say, and said, "Okay, let's go. Dora, as always, you're first."

I guessed that maybe things hadn't changed that much, because I went for the biggest present I could see. It stood as tall as my waist and was twice as wide as me. It wasn't wrapped all that neatly, so I knew it wasn't from Mom.

"To Dora, from Dad," I read from the tag. I tore off the wrapping paper and opened the plain box to find a bunch of crumpled up newspaper.

"Newspaper! Just what I always wanted!" I exclaimed.

"Ha ha, Dora. You're a real comedian," Dad said. "Just open it already."

I started digging through the newspaper. And digging. And digging. I was surrounded by a pile of newspaper balls, and still there was no present. When I had all the newspaper out, I saw sitting at the bottom of the box, a little package of mints. My eyes instantly filled up with tears.

There could have been a brand-new MacIntosh computer in there. There could have been a TV, but there was nothing that would have been more special to me than that little roll of mints and the memory of my father and his Certs.

1975

I get up late one morning and hear Daddy leaving while I am still in my room.

"Daddy! Wait!" I yell as I pull on my new bathrobe and run down the stairs, almost bumping into Tommy, who is on his way up.

I jump off the bottom step and into my father's arms.

"Well, good morning to you, sleepyhead. I didn't think you were going to get out of bed all day," he says, hugging me.

"I have school today, Daddy. Of course, I was getting out of bed," as I say this I rub my hands across his dress shirt pocket and feel the roll of Certs.

"Daddy?" I ask.

"Yes, Princess?"

"Can I have a mint?"

"That depends," he says, tapping his cheek.

"A kiss for a Certs!" I yell, and throw my arms around his neck, giving him a big kiss on the cheek. He puts me down and takes the mints out of his pocket. He opens the end of the roll and holds it toward me. I carefully take one out and pop it in my mouth. Then I run upstairs to get ready for school. I didn't even like his mints, they burned my mouth, but I loved the "kiss for a mint" game I play with my Daddy almost every day.

"Dora!" he shouts before I am halfway up the stairs. "Come back down here. Rainy! Come here!"

When Mommy comes into the room she doesn't give me her standard daily greeting, "Good morning, Sunshine!"

Instead, she looks at me and screams. It freaks me out. There must be something about the way I look that tells her what happened last night.

I look down at myself, my stomach, my legs, my feet. I don't see anything.

"What?" I ask, panic in my voice.

"Your ear!" she shouts. "What happened to your ear?"

For the first time, I realize my right ear is sore. I put my hand up to it and it feels crusty.

"I don't know! What's the matter with it?"

"I have an early meeting…" Dad begins.

"Go ahead, James. It's alright, I've got it."

Mom drags me into the bathroom and has me sit on the toilet lid. She gets cotton balls and some medicine from the cabinet. She wets the cotton balls and wipes my ear. It is really cold and it hurts really bad.

"Ouch, that hurts!" I howl. The mint flies out of my mouth and lands on the floor.

"Oh, my goodness, Dora, your earring is gone! Your hole is totally ripped open!"

I pull away from her and get up from the toilet to go look in the mirror. She hadn't cleaned all of the blood off yet, but it was enough to see that my earring hole is torn, right to the end of my ear. It looks really bad and really gross.

I am relieved though because I knew it must have happened in the night, but it doesn't give anything away.

My secret is still safe.

Chapter 14

1982

After all the Christmas festivities were over, like opening presents, going to church, and eating dinner, Pat and Donny took off to their friend's house. I was sitting in the living room, flipping through the channels, trying to find something to watch. It's a Wonderful Life was on practically every channel and I sure didn't want to watch it again. I had already seen it like a million times.

Mom came in and asked, "Dora, do you remember mine and Dad's friends, the Andersons?"

"I dunno. Maybe. Why?" I asked.

"They invited us over for a little while. Do you want to come? They have a daughter and she is only a couple years younger than you."

"Nah, I'll stay here, if that's okay," I said.

"Are you sure, Sweetie? I don't want to leave you here alone. Let me tell your father we'll go over another time," she said.

"Mom, seriously, it's fine. Go, have fun with your friends. Maybe I'll give Olivia a call and see if she wants to come over and watch a movie."

"Alright, that's a good idea. We won't be late, I promise. Give me a kiss," she said, coming over to me and hugging and kissing me. "Merry Christmas, Sweetie. I love you."

"I love you, too, Mom."

Dad stuck his head in the doorway. "You ready, ladies? I don't want to be out too late. I have work in the morning."

"Dora's going to stay home," my mother told him.

"Are you sure, Princess?" Dad asked.

"I'll see if Olive Oyl wants to come hang out." I tapped my check. "A kiss for a mint?"

Dad came over and gave me a kiss, but when I tried to give him a mint he said, "That's alright. That was a free one. I've got my own."

After they left I tried Olivia but she still had company. I felt a little pang of jealousy. Both sets of my grandparents had died and my mother was an only child. My dad had one brother but they had a fight when I was a kid and they didn't talk, so we didn't have anyone to invite over on holidays. Mom always said that was why she had so many kids. She felt like she missed out on not having a big family.

I wished I had gone with my parents after all. I gave up on the TV and started to wander around upstairs. I went into Donny's room and almost barfed at the smell of rotten food and sweaty basketball clothes. I snooped around his desk and checked out his papers from school. He was doing great. Most every assignment he got back had an A on it.

There was a paper pinned to his cork board that said, "My Goals: 1. Do really good in school 2. Check out law schools and get into the best one 3. Get a job as Assistant D.A. 4. Become D.A. 5. Become Attorney General."

I was impressed. By the looks of his room, I would have thought his only goal would have been to contract the Bubonic Plague.

Jim and Pat's room was cleaned out of all their stuff, but Dad was obviously using it for storage. There were boxes and furniture piled in there.

I turned across the hall from their room and in front of me was a closed door. Tommy's room. I knew that after he died, Mom had just shut his door and never went back in. There was a possibility that Dad had cleaned it out since Mom and I moved, but I doubted it. Most likely it was exactly the same way it was when he left there for the last time.

I put my hand on the doorknob and slowly turned it. I peeked before I went in and saw that I was right. The room was exactly the same. His bed was still made even.

I shut the door behind me and walked over to his bed, where I sat and looked around. The room was neat, it was left back in the day when Mom was like the cleaning Gestapo. She checked our rooms every morning before we left for school to make sure we had made our beds and put our dirty clothes in the hamper. His room didn't smell stale like I expected it to. It had been closed up almost as long as mine had been. I could actually still smell a fleeting scent of the Brut cologne he always wore.

I flopped back on his bed.

"Oh, Tommy, why did you do it? You were my big brother and I needed you."

I rolled over on my side and noticed a crumpled up piece of paper under his bureau. I dropped onto the floor, crawled over, and stretched out on the floor, reaching under the bureau for the paper. I had to reposition myself a couple of times, till I could actually reach it. Tommy's bureau was huge. When I finally got it, I sat up and un-crumbled it.

What I saw confused me. It made absolutely no sense. It was Tommy's signature, written over and over, like he was trying to practice to get it perfect. I used to do that in third grade, when I first learned cursive. Tommy had only been in this room for a couple years before he died, he used to share with Pat, so I doubted it was something that had been hanging around since he was a little kid. I crumbled it back up and raced downstairs to the woodstove.

As scared as I was to open the door, I did and threw the paper inside. I stood there with the door open and watched as it burned to ash, then slammed the door shut and locked it. I had no idea why, but I felt better with it gone.

I checked the clock and figured it would be an hour or so before my parents got back, so I chanced sneaking into Tommy's room again. I figured being in his room, around his things, smelling his cologne, I might remember something important. Even though I'd had more memories about my brother, I felt there is still something missing and I want to know what it is. I slipped back in his room, and closing the door behind me, I went back and sat on his bed.

I closed my eyes for a minute and took a deep breath. When I opened my eyes again, I was looking right at the Jaws movie poster hanging on his wall.

1975

Mommy drops me and my brothers off at the movie theater to see Jaws. I really, really want to see it and I almost don't get to go. My brothers are going to see it and I want to go with them. Mommy says I can't, she thinks I'm too little and it will be too scary for me – but my Daddy talks her into letting me go.

"How can you not let her see it?" he asks her. "She was in it, but she can't see it? Just let her. She knows it's just a movie."

My Mommy says that fine, I can go but that my Daddy is going to have to sit up with me all night when I am awake and screaming my head off from nightmares. Mommy and my brothers and I were all extras in the movie. I don't remember being in because I was only four, but Daddy is right. I know it's just a movie.

After the movie gets out we walk up the street to Cozy's and my brothers buy me an ice cream. We walk down the alley, eat our cones and talk about the movie. We go through Ocean Park on what I think is just a walk. As we walk and chat about the movie, I feel really grown-up. My brothers ask me what I thought about certain parts of the movie and really listen to my answers.

Even though whenever I walk into a room they would always stop talking and then talk about whatever I had to say, it never seemed as though they are really listening to me. This is probably the closest I ever felt to them and I am so proud. As we walk I hardly pay any attention to where we are going until I realize we are at the dock.

"So," Jim asks. "You weren't even scared a little bit, Dora?"

"No, I know it was all make believe," I answer him.

"Yeah, the movie was make-believe, but sharks aren't," Pat says.

"I know that," I say. "I'm not stupid."

"Didn't they make the movie based on a true story about a little girl who got eaten by a shark right here?" Donny asks.

"Actually, yeah, I think so. But she was only like seven or eight. Hey, Dora, how old are you?" Jim asks.

"I'm seven," I whisper.

"Uh oh. You better stay out of the water," Jim says, laughing.

"Cut it out! You guys are just trying to scare me!"

"Yeah, quit it, you guys," Tommy says.

"Shut up, Tommy," Jim says. "You know what else I heard? They've actually seen some Great Whites around here, but just like in the movie they're keeping it secret so they don't scare away the tourists."

"You're lying!" I yell, backing away.

"Okay," Jim says, grabbing me around the waist and carrying me to the edge of the dock. "If we're lying then you won't mind taking a swim."

He puts me down in front of the rail and Pat comes over. They each grab one of my arms and lift me up so my stomach is on the rail and I am looking down into the water. I kick at them but Donny grabs my feet and holds them tight.

"So help me," Tommy says in a voice that sounds like he is growling. "If she goes into that water, I'll kick all three of your asses and then I'll tell Mom and Dad."

Donny lets go of my legs when Tommy puts him in what they call a choke hold on the wrestling shows they like to watch.

There must be something in Tommy's voice that really makes Jim and Pat believe that he could beat them up, even though they are bigger than him, because Jim and Pat lower me from the railing and put me back on the dock. Tommy lets go of Donny's neck and pushes him down. I run into Tommy's arms and he hugs me tight.

"Chill out, man, we were just messing with her. We weren't really gonna do it," Jim says.

Tommy doesn't answer him. He just picks me up and walks toward the beginning of the dock. I wrap my arms around his neck and my legs around his waist, squeezing as tight as I can to stop myself from shaking.

Tommy carries me all the way back to the theater, where Mom is supposed to pick us up. Tommy doesn't tell on Jim, Pat, and Donny. I don't either. I don't know why I don't, I usually love to get them in trouble. Maybe it is because I know that if Tommy hadn't been there, they would have thrown me in and even though there are no sharks in there to eat me, I most likely would have hit a piling and broke my neck.

I couldn't tell my parents that my brothers meant to kill me.

Chapter 15

1983

When the regular basketball season ended for the year, the girls' team missed going to the playoffs by one game, but the boys' team made it. Since Jared had made the winning basket in their last game, he was the hero of the school. Invitations to all kinds of parties started flooding in and he invited me to go along with him to every one of them.

I was never really into the whole partying scene and didn't realize the extent of it on the Island. Every weekend there was a party at somebody's house, sometimes two. It seemed like an awful lot of parents went off-Island and trusted their kids to not have parties. That was pretty much a big mistake.

There was this whole sex thing that went on at these house parties. It was never really talked about, at least during the party, but by Monday morning it would be the talk of the school. Unlike junior high parties where spin the bottle and 7 minutes in heaven were played for everybody to witness, the high school party sex scene was hush-hush. There was always a room set aside, either the kid who was having the party's room or his or her parents' room. Two people, sometimes even three, would just disappear from the party for a while and nobody said anything.

I wasn't sure if it was something that was planned ahead of time or if it just happened spontaneously. I didn't know because Jared never said anything about it to me. He was a perfect gentleman and never tried to push me into doing anything I didn't want to do.

One night we went to a party at this kid Alex's house. The boys' team had just won their first playoff game, and of course Jared was the hero again. Alex wasn't on the basketball team or anything and he was kind of a goofy kid, but he sure threw a killer party. He had an older brother who watched him whenever his parents went away, but unbeknownst to them, for the payment of a case of beer, his big brother would supply him with a party's worth of booze and turn a blind eye to whatever Alex did.

When we got to the front door, Alex had people there collecting money, an entrance fee, they called it. Jared and I got hustled in without getting charged and right away I lost Jared in the crowd of his adoring fans. The music was playing so loud I couldn't just hear it, I could feel it vibrating in my bones. The smell of beer was so strong, I wondered if you could get drunk just from breathing the air.

I was walking through the living room, looking for the bathroom when I spotted Stacy across the room. I tried to duck behind a crowd of kids who were dancing and spilling their beers all over each other, but it was too late. She saw me and came pushing through the crowd.

"Can I talk to you for a minute?" she screamed in my face.

I pretended like I didn't hear her, "What?"

"I want to talk to you!" She grabbed my arm and pulled me back toward the front door.

I looked around desperately for Jared, but I didn't see him anywhere. I had a bad feeling that everyone at the party would be so drunk, nobody would notice what was happening. In the morning Alex's parents would come home and find me in a bloody heap on their front lawn.

The only reason why I let her drag me out was because at least she was alone. I could defend myself against just her. When we got outside, she continued holding onto my arm and dragged me around the side of the house.

My heart skipped a beat when I saw that Brandy and Laurie were already there.

"Christ, it's loud in there," Stacy complained.

"What do you want, Stacy?" I asked.

"We just wanted to talk to you. We felt bad about that day in the hallway," she said.

I couldn't help being suspicious. Stacy never felt bad about anything.

"That's okay. I'm not worried about it." I turned to head back into the house.

"Hold on, Dora. That's not all we wanted to talk to you about," Brandy said. I knew it.

"What's up?" I asked.

"Well, we just wanted to ask you, because we didn't want you to be upset…but Laurie kind of likes Jared and she wants to ask him out," Stacy said.

"What?" I asked, the shock I felt clearly coming out in my voice.

"Since you guys are breaking up and all, I just figured…but really, if it will bother you that much, I won't," Laurie said.

"What are you talking about? Breaking up?" I asked.

Stacy dramatically covered her mouth. "Oh, no. You didn't know?"

"No, I didn't," I said.

"Oh, God, I'm wicked sorry. I thought he already talked to you. He's been telling everyone else. I thought for sure you knew," Stacy tried to sound like she really was sorry, but I was pretty sure she was trying her hardest not to crack up.

"You can only be a tease with a guy for so long. If you don't give it up sooner or later, they're gonna dump you. Geez, didn't you learn anything from hanging out with us?" Brandy asked.

I turned and ran back to the house. I couldn't be sure because the music got loud as I got closer to the house, but

I was pretty sure I could hear the three of them laughing. It took me a while to find Jared in the crowd.

But when I finally did, he asked, "Where have you been? I've been looking for you everywhere. My little sister is sick and my mother needs her car back to take her to the hospital. Do you want to stay? Or I can give you a ride."

My heart was racing and there was a huge lump of regret in my throat. Was this it? Was this how he was going to break up with me? Tell me his sister was sick and then on the way home, tell me that it was over? I wasn't sure what to say.

"It's okay with me if you want to stay. I probably won't come back, though. Most likely I'll end up going to the ER."

This was it. I had to make my choice, so I made it. "No, I'll go. I wouldn't want to stay without you, anyway."

When we got in the car, I knew I would have to just blurt it out, or I would lose my nerve, "Joe's party is tomorrow night, right?"

"Actually, Dora, I wanted to talk to you about that," he said.

Shit, I thought, Stacy was telling the truth. She was being her regular old nasty self by telling me like that, but she wasn't lying.

"I'm not sure if I'm gonna be able to go."

"That's too bad," I said.

"Why?" he asked.

"I was thinking that, uhm, maybe you could, uhm, ask Joe if we could use his parents' room for a while, you know, uhm, during the party."

He glanced over at me. "Are you sure, Dora? I don't want you to feel like you have to or something. I'm okay with waiting until you're sure you're ready."

Was he telling the truth? Or was Stacy, and this was just some guy way to get girls into bed and make it look like they weren't the ones who were pushing it? It didn't matter. I had to do it. I loved him and I didn't want to lose him.

"I'm sure, Jared. I'm ready."

"Okay, then, I'll talk to Joe. But it still depends on my uncle, if I'm even going or not," he said.

"Your uncle?" I asked.

"Yeah, that's what I was going to tell you. My uncle might need me to go off Island with him to check his rental house on the Cape. There's something wrong with the roof or something, and he asked me to come up and help him fix it, if my dad can't go. I'll know tomorrow."

Jared ended up not having to go help his uncle and by the time we got to Joe's party, I was so nervous, I didn't think I'd be able to go through with it. I wasn't much of a drinker, but I had plenty to drink that night. I had to, just to stop my hands from shaking.

By the time Jared grabbed my hand and led me down the hall to Joe's parents' bedroom, I could barely even walk.

We went into the room and Jared sat me down on the bed. We started kissing and I felt like I was doing the right thing. Jared moved onto the bed and gently pushed me down. He started kissing me again and soon both of our pants were off and he was on top of me. He was just about to enter me and that was it. Something snapped in me and I started screaming. I pushed Jared off, scrambled off the bed, pulled on my pants, and ran out the door. Jared found me a few minutes later, sitting behind a tree in Joe's yard, crying the hiccupy kind of cries that babies do when they are really hysterical, deep in another memory I didn't want to have.

1975

My Mommy goes to ceramics and my Daddy is in his office doing some work that he needs to have done for the morning. My brothers are watching a movie in the living room. I go to bed early and fell asleep quickly.

I wake up sometime later when my door opens. I think it must be my mother checking in on me, but then the door closes and someone is still in the room. I hear somebody walk over to my bed and then I hear the sound of a zipper being undone.

I don't know what to do, so I stay very still and hope I am having a bad dream. I feel my bed move as somebody climbs in under the covers with me. I want to scream but he clamps his hand over my mouth and whispers in my ear,

"Shhh, Princess, shhh."

I realize he is not wearing any clothes and I don't know what he is doing.

"Just close your eyes and imagine a horse, a beautiful horse with a beautiful princess riding it. Oh, look, she's wearing such a pretty gown! Just think about that, okay? Everything will be fine."

When he pulls up my nightie and gets on top of me, I begin to understand. What he does hurts so bad and I want to scream, but I can't because of his hand over my mouth. I bite down as hard as I can, but even as blood fills my mouth, he doesn't let go.

He jerks and twists on top of me, my body screams with the agony that my mouth cannot. He collapses on the bed next to me, breathing heavily, and then he gets up and puts his clothes back on.

Before he leaves, he comes over to the bed and whispers, "Don't you tell anyone, Dora, because if you do, I'll tell everyone the truth about Piggily-Wiggily."

Chapter 16

1983

When I woke up in the morning after Joe's party, my head was pounding and it didn't help that Mom and Dad were in the living room, yelling. Great, I thought, they're right back to the way they used to be.

I went into the bathroom and knelt down in front of the toilet until I was sure I wasn't gonna barf. I found a bottle of aspirin in the medicine chest and took three. Then I went out to the living room.

Dad was sitting on the couch, with his hands on his face. Mom was sitting on the arm of the couch, rubbing his back. My first thought was at least they're not fighting and it was quickly replaced by fear. My father was crying. I didn't think I had ever seen him cry.

"What's the matter?" I asked, my voice shaky with panic.

"Your father's brother had a heart attack, Dora," my mother answered for him.

"Uncle Les?" I asked. I barely even remembered him. "Is he..?"

"He's in intensive care, but they think he's going to be alright."

"What am I supposed to do, Rainy? I haven't said a word to him in almost four years. I'm just supposed to show up there, like nothing ever happened?" Dad asked.

"That's what I would suggest," my mother said. "I'm getting dressed and going to the hospital to sit with Ginny."

"I don't know if I can do it," Dad said.

"James, there comes a time when you have to let things go. I think this is that time. If your brother dies in that hospital, you'll feel guilty for the rest of your life."

"I didn't do anything to him, Rainy" Dad said.

"I know, but now you need to forgive him for what he did."

"I think it's gone beyond that at this point."

"You do what you want, James. I'm going. I'll be ready in ten minutes."

Mom got up and headed to the bathroom and Dad buried his face in his hands, letting out a sob. I stood in the doorway, unsure about what I should do. I finally turned and went back into my room, closing my door softly behind me.

1980

Daddy and his brother Les used to be very close. Uncle Les and his wife Ginny lived up-Island and hardly a week passed when they didn't get together and do something. Sometimes they all went out, or Aunt Ginny cooked for my parents, or Mom cooked for them.

At times we had family dinners and we went to their house or Uncle Les and Aunt Ginny brought their daughters Sierra and Corrine to our house.

The last time they see each other is at our house. We are having a family dinner, so their girls come with them. I am eleven, almost a teenager, and there is no way I am going to hang out with Sierra and Corrine, who are only eight and nine. They bring a box of Barbie dolls with them and are sitting on the rug of Mom's special room playing while the adults sit around and talk. I am kind of jealous that they get to hang around in there, but not jealous enough to go play with them.

When they first come, Mom interrogates them and inspects the shoe box they brought for anything that could ruin her expensive furniture.

"Do you have any paints or crayons?"

"No, Auntie," they answer in unison.

"What about scissors or anything else that's sharp?"

"I made sure they didn't put anything like that in the box," Aunt Ginny says.

"Okay," Mom says. "You can play in here, but you have to promise to clean everything up before we eat, okay?"

"We will, Auntie," in unison again. I wonder if they had practiced.

I go upstairs to my room and wait to get called down for dinner. My brothers are in the living room watching TV and Uncle Les goes in there every few minutes and sucks down a beer, since there is no food or drink allowed in the sitting room. By the time Mom calls us all for dinner, Uncle Les is pretty well sloshed.

The first part of dinner goes okay but Uncle Les continues drinking and like my mother always says, his tongue gets away from him when he drinks too much.

"So, James, you almost had yourself a whole basketball team here. If Dora had been a boy, you could've started a team!"

"Girls play basketball too," Mom says.

"But Dora doesn't, does she?"

"No, she was on the swim team, and I'm pretty sure she's thinking about joining it again," Dad answers.

"Swim team?" Uncle Les says, laughing. "Is swimming even a real sport?"

"It most certainly is!" Mom says a little too loudly.

"More so than what you do, Les. What is it again, golf?"

"James…" my mother says, warning in her voice.

"Doesn't matter anyway," Uncle Les says. "Since that boy of yours offed himself, you're down to just four anyway."

"Les!" Aunt Ginny shouts, jumping to her feet.

I have never seen my father's face turn so red.

"Lester, I think it's time you packed up your family and left."

I glance over at my mother, expecting her to dispute what my father said, but she just sits there with tears in her eyes.

Uncle Les, Aunt Ginny, and the girls all get up, gather their stuff, and leave. My family continues to sit at the table, nobody eating, nobody talking.

After a few minutes my father stands up, wipes his face and throws his napkin down on his plate.

"Well, I guess this dinner is over then. Wouldn't you say? You kids clean up the table. Your mother and I are going upstairs."

Mom and Dad never go out with Uncle Les and Aunt Ginny again.

Chapter 17

1983

When Mom and Dad went to the hospital to be with Aunt Ginny, they brought the girls to stay at the house with me. I really wanted to go back to our house, but if I had to stay at my father's house, I was glad to at least have company.

It had been four years since I had last seen them, and I barely recognized them.

If I had run into them anywhere besides my own living room, I suspected I wouldn't have even known they were my cousins.

My mother ordered us pizza for dinner and we sat in the kitchen and ate it, without talking too much.

Then Corrine told her sister to go into the living room and watch TV.

"Where can I go to smoke?" Corrine asked me as soon as Sierra was in the other room.

"Smoke?" I asked, incredulous. "You're twelve years old!"

"Actually," she said, "I'm thirteen."

"You're still too young to smoke. Besides, your father just had a heart attack."

"My father didn't have a heart attack because he smoked. He had a heart attack 'cause he's a hundred pounds overweight and drinks like a fucking fish."

"Still...smoking is bad for you," I said.

"Are you gonna lecture me, or tell me where I can go?"

"Go out on the porch," I suggested.

"I can't. Sierra might see me and besides your parents could come back any minute."

I shrugged. "Go out on the back porch then."

"It's too scary back there." Corrine said.

I couldn't argue with her on that point. It was all woods behind the house and it was a dark night. I wouldn't be caught dead on the porch after the sun went down.

"I suppose you could go up to the attic and go out on the roof like my brothers used to do to smoke."

"Your brothers smoked?" she asked.

"Yeah, why?"

"I can't wait to tell Francis that one!" Corrine started laughing.

"Who's Francis?" I asked.

"My older brother."

"You have an older brother? How come I never met him?" I asked.

"Dad knocked up some summer chick when he was still in high school and he lives off-Island with her. But whenever your brothers did anything, my father would be like, 'Why can't you be like Jim?' Or Pat, or whoever just did something great. He'll love to hear that they smoked and your mother didn't know."

"That's awful that your father did that," I said.

"My mother does the same thing to me. About you."

"About me?"

"Like, totally. When you made the honor roll and then the basketball team, that's all I heard about for weeks. 'Why can't you be like your cousin Dora? Dora did this, and Dora did that. I don't really want to admit it, but I kinda hated you. You set this standard that I could never quite reach. I would have been on the honor roll, except for algebra. It's not my fault there's a gazillion formulas and I mix them up."

I told her what my teacher let us do.

"Are you serious?" Corrine asked. "Unbelievable."

"How does your mother know what I've been doing anyway?" I asked. "Our parents haven't talked for years."

"Are you kidding? Our mothers go out for coffee like once a week."

"My mother never told me that. She probably didn't want Dad to know," I said.

"Why would she tell you anyway? The only reason why I knew was so my mother could compare us. Anyway, will you come on the roof with me?"

No way, I thought. "I'll show you, but I'm not going up there."

"Why not?" she asked.

I had no reason to give her, so I just shrugged and led her to the attic. I followed her up the stairs, but I stopped when we got to the top.

When she reached the top step, I expected her to trip, but she didn't. She continued over to the window.

"Right here?" she asked.

"Yup."

"Please come with me," she opened the window and climbed out on the roof.

"No, I'll stay here."

"You're weird," she said.

I got a good idea, "I'll stay to be the look out, in case your sister comes looking for you."

"That's actually smart. You sure she can't see me from inside the house?" she asked.

"I'm sure." I sat on the top step and looked toward the bottom of the stairs.

Corinne sat on the roof right in front of the window and kept one hand inside with a death-grip on the windowsill. She was still complaining about her teacher and saying that maybe we should get mine to call hers.

I just answered with a series of "uh huh's" when it seemed appropriate, but honestly I wasn't even listening to her.

I was focusing all my attention at the bottom of the stairs, willing myself not to look toward the left where the bureau was with my old dollhouse tucked behind it.

After a couple of minutes of struggling with myself, my will power gave out and I glanced over. The first thing I saw was the big ugly bureau I used to hide behind.

I see the pile of tools I used to work on my dollhouse, which was gone: a roll of Bicentennial eagle wallpaper, a pair of scissors, a bottle of school glue, and a crumpled-up glue-covered square of eagle wallpaper.

But most of all, like everything else lately, there was a memory waiting in that pile.

1975

I am in the attic playing, well actually working, in the corner behind a bureau where my father stored my old dollhouse. I had gotten it for Christmas the year before. My father put it all together but it never got anything done to it after that.

It isn't that I don't want to finish it, but my parents won't buy me what I need to do it, so I am trying to cover the walls with paper towel wallpaper and it isn't working.

I wipe off the glue with tissue, and I get frustrated because I am getting more tissue on the walls than I am getting glue on the tissue. I mutter under my breath, but I stop when I hear my brothers come up the stairs.

It is only Jim, Pat, and Donny. Tommy is in jail. They open the window and climb out on the roof.

They all sit down and Jim lights a cigarette. He smokes it for a minute and then hands it to Pat. I slink back into the shadows.

"So, what do you guys think?" Jim asks. "Did he rape her?"

"No way!" Pat howls. "He said he never touched that girl."

"What did he say?"

"He said whenever he went over to his friend Philip's house she was always hanging around, trying to come on to him." Pat says, blowing smoke rings

"So, he fucked her?" Jim asks, taking the cigarette back from Pat.

"No way. She was his best friend's little sister. A little kid with a crush on him."

"Why would she say it then?" Jim asks.

"Maybe to get him in trouble 'cause he wouldn't," Pat suggests, shrugging his shoulders..

"She's in my school," Donny informs them. "And she says it never even happened."

"Then how come he's in jail, huh?"

"Cause her father called the police. He came home early and caught Tommy climbing out the window, half undressed. When he asked Tommy's friend, he said he was in the bathroom and didn't know nothing," Jim tells everyone.

"And the girl really said it didn't happen?" Pat asks Donny.

"Yeah, but they don't believe her," Donny answers.

"So, they both say it didn't happen, I don't understand why he's in jail then," Pat complains.

"She didn't say it didn't happen to the police, she said he made her do it."

"And cause the father found a used condom in her bedroom garbage and caught him going out her window. I think that's what they call 'probable cause,'" Jim states sarcastically.

"She said something that I don't want to tell you," Donny says quietly.

"Oh, you better tell us," Jim threatens, balling his fists in Donny's direction.

"I swore I wouldn't tell anyone. Philip will kill me. Besides, it's just something his sister said and I don't even know if it's true."

"I'll kill you if you don't tell, so what's the difference?" Jim threatens again.

"He wasn't fucking his sister. He was fucking Philip."

Jim howls with laughter. "Oh, shit!"

"Yeah, and Philip said they had to say it was her and that he would fuck them up if they told anyone what really happened. And then when her father asked her about it, she didn't want to get in trouble, so she said he raped her."

"We have to get Tommy to tell the truth," Jim says.

"No! You can't let anyone know I told you," Donny protests.

"You'd rather he went to jail?"

"Then get murdered by Philip, actually, yeah. Even Tommy isn't admitting what really happened. That must tell you something."

"Sorry, that ain't happening. If you gotta take a beatin' then you take it and you don't complain," Pat says.

"Tommy doesn't want anyone to know, either," Donny counters.

"Sure, he'd rather be known as a rapist than gay. I doubt that," Jim says, stubbing out the cigarette and lighting a new one.

"He doesn't want Ma and Dad to know for sure," Donny informs him.

"I just hope what you're saying is true. I've been kinda worried about Dora," Jim says. "I mean, what if that girl isn't even lying? What if he did rape her? How can we be sure he hasn't done the same thing to Dora?"

I want to jump up and scream that they should never, ever say those things about Tommy, but I can't give away my hiding place.

I can't let them know I am spying on them.

I have to bite down on my tongue to keep from screaming at the top of my lungs, because I think if I start, I won't ever be able to stop.

Chapter 18

1983

On the first Friday of February vacation I went and stayed at Dad's. None of my brothers were around and that was the only reason why I agreed to go.

After we ate lunch and Dad and I were doing the dishes, I decided to ask him about my name. I had asked Mom before, but she never really gave me an answer.

"So, how was it that you and Mom came up with the name Adorable for me, anyway?"

"You don't know this story?" he asked.

I shook my head.

"Your mother and I gave up thinking that we were ever going to have a girl. So, when she got pregnant with you, we only chose a boy's name."

"What was it?" I asked.

"Noah," he said.

"Oh, so by that logic, if I had been a boy, I would have had a normal name."

"What's wrong with Adorable?" he asked.

"I'm a person, Dad. Not an adjective."

"Do you want to hear the rest of the story?"

I nodded and Dad went on, "So, when you were born and the doctor said, 'It's a girl!' your mother and I looked at each other, surprised that you weren't a boy. They cleaned you up and handed you to your mother. I said, 'She's adorable,' and your mother said, 'She certainly isn't a Noah.' So, the name just kind of stuck."

"Jeez, Dad, you guys couldn't have thought about it a little longer and come up with a normal girl name?"

"We talked about a few names, but we kept going back to Adorable. It just seemed to fit the moment. And you. You were the most adorable baby I had ever seen."

"I suppose if you've got to have a stupid name, at least it's good that there's a story behind it."

"You think it's a stupid name? I think it's beautiful," Dad opined, handing me a dish to dry and put away.

"Of course, I thought it was stupid. I didn't let anyone call me anything but Dora since I was five years old."

"I just assumed you wanted a nickname, like your brothers."

I took a deep breath and regretted the words I said as soon as they came out of my mouth, "Dad, about my brothers…"

"What about them?"

What the hell did I think I was going to say anyway?

"Um, nothing, I was just wondering what they were all up to?"

After Dad and I finished the dishes, I went upstairs to take a nap before I had to get ready to go out with Jared. We were going out on a date that night, but he wouldn't tell me where he was taking me. He said it was a surprise and he wouldn't tell me no matter how much I begged him.

He showed up at five o'clock, right as I finished getting dressed. We drove up Vineyard Haven/West Tisbury Road and headed up Island. He still wouldn't tell me where we were going. We drove into Chilmark and then we pulled onto a long dirt driveway.

When he finally stopped the car, we were in front of a beautiful post and beam house that was made mostly out of glass.

"Where are we, Jared?" I asked, a little nervous.

"Don't worry," he said. "Come on."

We got out of the car and went up to the door. Jared rang the doorbell and we waited while we heard somebody with a thick Spanish accent calling out that she would be right there.

A tiny Hispanic woman dressed in a maid's outfit answered the door.

"Ah, Senor Jared, finally you are here! Come in!"

We stepped into the foyer and she put her hands out to take our jackets.

"Juanita, I would like to introduce my friend, Dora," Jared said.

"Nice to meet you. You need me to show you the way?" she asked as she hung our coats in a closet.

"I think I'm all set. Thank you, Senorita."

Jared led me through the most amazing house I had ever seen. Everything from the floors to the walls was made of marble or glass. I looked around in wonder and Jared finally grabbed my hand to make me move faster.

We walked through the whole house, went out the back door and walked across a little bridge that led to a gazebo.

Jared held the door open for me. "Ladies first."

I laughed and stepped into the cutest little building I had ever seen. It was made out of red wood and was entirely glassed in. The floor was tiled and there was a fireplace in the corner. with a cheery fire blazing and candles lit on wall sconces all around. There was a small round table set up right in the middle of the gazebo. It was covered with a white tablecloth and had flowers and lit candles set up on it.

Jared pulled out my chair for me. "Here you go, ma'am."

"Thank you," I said as I took my seat.

Jared grabbed a bottle of soda and two fancy crystal wine glasses from the bar and poured us each a glass. Juanita came in and put a plate of salad in front of each of us.

I was pretty confused about where we were and whose house it was. I was about to ask him what was going on when I spotted a flash of color out of the corner of my eye. I turned and for the first time realized that the gazebo was in the middle of a body of water.

Classical music started playing, and water began spraying up all around the gazebo like a giant fountain. Colors flashed and faded in time with the music, and the water kept the beat also.

When the music reached a crescendo the water would spray really high and then go back down when the music got quiet. It seemed like the water was dancing in tune to the music. It was the most amazing and beautiful thing I had ever seen in my life. We watched the show and ate our salads. It lasted for about fifteen minutes and then it was quiet and dark again.

"What was that?" I asked, breathless.

"The man who owns this house had it built for his wife. I guess they had seen something like it during a trip to Japan and she really loved it. They came home from the trip and she got sick, so he built it for her," Jared said, stacking up our salad plates.

"What happened to his wife?" I asked.

"She's in a nursing home off Island now. But he brings her back here whenever he can. She loves it here."

"I can see why. It's amazing. How did you know about it?"

Juanita came in and took away our salad plates and gave us plates with steak, potatoes, and a vegetable medley.

"My father's company built it for him. I told my father I wanted to do something special for you. He talked to the owner and they planned this all out," he said, cutting into his steak. "After what happened at Joe's party, I kind of felt like I owed you."

"You didn't owe me anything, Jared. I told you, it wasn't your fault. It was me. I...I just wasn't ready. Besides, I should be apologizing to you. I freaked and made you look like a jerk."

"Not really. Nobody even noticed, they were all so drunk. But I felt really bad about it. I really like you, Dora," he confessed, taking a bite of the steak..

"I promise. It had nothing to do with you. It's me," I said.

"You sure? Because I would never want to do anything to hurt you," he said, looking up at me.

I wanted to tell him the truth so bad that the words burned my throat. "Actually, Jared, if I tell you something…"

"Sure, anything, Dora."

I couldn't tell him though. It was a secret that I would have to take to the grave, "Nothing. Forget about it. I'm fine. I don't want to talk about it."

1976

"She needs to talk about it…" my mother says.

"That's the problem with you people and all this new-fangled crap. We all had problems when we were kids and our parents didn't take us to some quack to talk about them. We grew up just fine," Dad says.

I'm not spying on them. They are in the kitchen talking and I am in the coat closet outside the kitchen door. I like to go in there, curl up under the coats that never seem to stay hung up.

"Nothing like this certainly ever happened to me," Mom says.

"Not that you remember, anyway. It doesn't even matter, Rainy. She's young, she'll forget all about it. If you keep taking her to see these doctors you work for and they make her keep talking about it, she won't forget. Besides, you asked her about it, and she said that it didn't even happen, right?" Dad asks.

"Why would he say it then? Why would he leave it in his note?" I hear my mother crying.

"Why would he do anything that he did, Rainy? Why would he molest a little girl? Why would he blow his own head off? Does anything he did make sense? To you? To me? To anyone? Tell me, Rainy! If you can understand any of this, tell me! Because I really want to know!"

"I just want to take her a few more times. Dr. Hanson has been doing this therapy with her called 'guided imagery' and feels that Dora is responding really well. She says she's sure that we are really close to a breakthrough and that if anything has happened to Dora, we're getting close to the time it is going to come out. If nothing happened, fine, we won't take her again. If it did happen, the therapist can help her to make sense of it," my Mommy says.

"Don't you mean rehash it? That's all these quacks do. Make kids talk about things over and over, till they actually do go crazy and then they have to keep going back. Meanwhile, the unsuspecting parents pay for the nut doctor's kid's college tuition! Besides, Rainy, he's gone! Dead and gone! Whatever happened is over, it's in the past! Leave it there!"

"I'm sorry, James. I don't agree with you on this one."

"Then I guess we're at the clichéd 'agree to disagree' because my decision is final. She is not going to talk to anyone anymore and that's it. Understand?"

I hear Mom run out of the kitchen and up the stairs.

I curl up in a ball deep under the coats. I want to stay here forever. I'll be safe here.

Because you are wrong, Daddy. Tommy never, ever touched me.

Jim did.

Chapter 19

1983

On Saturday at the end of vacation Mom told me that at four o'clock I needed to be ready to leave because she and Dad had a surprise for me. I pretty much already knew what it was – the house was done and Dad had moved in.

There were two other building lots that were available for Pat, Donny or me; whoever wanted one. Jim had bought one of the lots at the old house and was planning on building a house there in the next couple of years.

When we got to the new house, Dad came around from the backyard and called us over. We parked behind another car that wasn't familiar to me and then got out and walked to the back of the house.

Uncle Les, Aunt Ginny, and the girls were sitting at a table that was set up on the patio. Aunt Ginny got up and she and my mother hugged. Then Mom went over to where Uncle Les was sitting and hugged him. She kissed the girls on the tops of their heads, while Aunt Ginny came over and hugged me.

"Go give your uncle a hug," Aunt Ginny said. "He's still supposed to be taking it easy."

I hugged my uncle and smiled at the girls and then went over to my father and gave him a huge hug.

"How's my princess?" he asked. "Let's go, I'll give you a tour of the house."

It was a three bedroom. Dad explained to me that the big one upstairs was the master bedroom, one downstairs was going to be a guest room for Pat and Donny when they came to visit, now that Donny had moved off-Island to be closer to his school, and the other one was mine. He brought me over to the room that was right at the bottom of the stairs. The door was shut.

"You ready?" he asked.

I nodded and he pushed the door open. The room was unfinished.

"Wow," I said. "It's huge!"

"I have your canopy bed and all the matching furniture stored in the garage," Dad told me. "I went off Island last week and priced the wallpaper and rug to make this room just like your old one. Well, pretty much, they didn't have the exact same wallpaper, but it was close."

"I think I would rather have something totally new, if you don't mind," I told him.

"Whatever you want, Princess, it's your room."

We went out back to the patio. Sierra and Corrine were setting the table with plastic plates and silverware that they were taking out of a picnic basket. Mom and Aunt Ginny were over at the grill, Mom was taking lobster out of a pot on one of the burners and Aunt Ginny was taking corn from another.

Dad went over to the grill, and lifting the top, took out foil-wrapped potatoes. They brought the food over to the table and we all got served two lobsters; well, all of us except for Sierra who brought a hamburger that her mother cooked on the grill for her. She said she refused to eat anything that had eyes.

I refrained from pointing out the fact that the cow had eyes, because I knew what she meant. You didn't have to look at them when you were eating a burger.

"This is lovely," Mom said, cracking open a lobster claw with her hands. "Dora, make sure you thank Auntie and Uncle for bringing these beautiful lobsters."

Something occurred to me then.

"Uncle Les, you have a lobster boat?" I asked.

"I do. I'm not currently running it. My oldest son is staying with us and working for me until my doc gives me the ok to go back to work."

Then I asked him the name of his boat and he told me, even though I was pretty sure I already knew. When I was a little girl my mother always talked about fairies. She always asked the "Parking Fairy" to help her find a space.

Whenever she was cleaning she would joke that the "Cleaning Fairy" didn't show up again. She also talked about the "Cooking Fairy" and the "Laundry Fairy". I asked her once where all the lobsters in the fridge came from.

When she answered me, I heard, "The Lobster Fairy." What she really said was, "The Lobster Ferry" - the name of Uncle Les' lobster boat.

When Mom and I were driving home she asked me, "What's the matter? I thought you would be more excited about the house."

"I am. I'm just thinking. Mom, look out!"

A beautiful fluffy all white dog darted across the road right in front of us. Mom slammed on her brakes and put her hand up across my chest.

"Sorry," Mom said sheepishly as she removed her arm. "Just a reflex."

The dog reached the other side of the road and went into the woods. Mom started moving again.

"Wait! Shouldn't we go back and try to catch him? What if he gets hit by a car?"

"I'm not going to try to catch it. I hate those dogs."

I looked at my mother surprised. She never used "hate," saying it was a horrible word.

"You don't remember Chip?" Mom asked.

"I do. But what does that dog have to do with Chip?"

When I was little Dad bought a Chinese Pug for my mother. They named him "Chipper" because he was so energetic and we called him Chip for short. It was a source of endless entertainment to straighten out his curly tail, because then he would see it and go around and around in a circle trying to catch it.

Mom said that he was so ugly that he was cute and Dad said he had a flat face because he chased parked cars. I guess I was a pretty gullible kid, because I used to watch him closely in the driveway to make sure he didn't run into Mom or Dad's cars.

Chip followed me to school one morning and I got to bring him inside until my mother could come and get him. Everyone crowded around me, wanting to pet him. I loved all the attention I got that day, so I brought Chip to school with me a couple more times. I would let him out of the house before breakfast and when I left for school I would walk a little ways from the house and call his name. He would come running and follow me.

Whenever we passed a neighbor's house, who I thought might be up and paying attention, I would turn, point down the road and shout, "Go home, Chip! Stop following me!"

Chip would listen, but when I got past the house I would call him again and he would come running. This happened three or four times and by the time we got to school poor Chip must have been so confused.

"That dog was a husky. They're very violent dogs. One of our neighbors had one, and he killed Chip."

1975

Tommy is in jail and I am sad and scared. I wake up the morning after he gets arrested and it is nice outside, so I decide to go to the woods and check on my Indian village. I check on the blueberry bushes to see if there are any buds, and there aren't. I can't wait for them to grow.

I love it when Mommy sends me out to pick a basket and then we make blueberry pancakes or muffins together for breakfast.

I walk deeper into the woods, carrying a stick and whacking the bushes on both sides of the path, making the dead leaves fall off. I have to pass my brothers' fort to get to my village. It is a fort on the ground made out of a bunch of doors that they nailed to trees to make a big circle. There is one door that isn't nailed so they can use it to get in and out. I think the inside must be wicked awesome, but I don't know for sure because I'm not allowed to go in.

I hear my brothers yelling and laughing inside the fort. I get as close as I can without being seen and crawl on my belly to hide under some thick bushes. I can see the fort but am pretty sure they can't see me. I can still hear them perfectly though.

"Yaw! Yaw!" I hear Donny yell. "Kick it here!"

I hear some kind of a yelp, but I don't know what it is because I've never heard anything like it before. All I know is that even though it is warm out, a chill passes through my body and goose-bumps pop up on my arms.

"Come on, you mangy thing!" Pat shouts.

Donny and Jim laugh and I hear that squeal again. I still don't know what it is. I also don't know what "mangy" meant and I can't look it up in my dictionary because my Mommy took it away from me for a week. Donny told her I was looking up dirty words.

"Oh shit," Jim said, and then laughs. "Now you did it!"

"Kick it! It's fine!" Donny says.

I stay under the bushes for a long time listening to them shout and laugh. I am frozen to my spot under the bushes when they finally come out. I can't see them because the door that moves is on the other side of the fort and they don't pass by me when they leave.

"Dude, don't worry about it. I totally got this," Jim says as they run away deeper into the woods. "I have the greatest plan."

I stay under the bushes for a very long time, afraid to move. I'm not sure, but I think I fall asleep for a little while, because I feel groggy and dizzy. I don't go to check on my village, but when I get up, I crawl out from under the bushes and follow the path back to my house.

I find my mother crying in her sitting room, with my brothers all around her. Jim stands next to her, patting her back. Donny sits on one side and holds her hand, and Pat sits on the other and rests his head on her shoulder.

"Don't worry, Ma," Jim says. "The dog catcher'll take care of it. Dad'll make sure."

"What happened?" I ask.

My head feels fuzzy. I want to throw up but I'm not sure why.

My mother looks up at me and wipes her nose with a tissue that Jim hands to her before she answers me.

"That horrible dog, that husky that lives on the other side of the woods killed poor Chip. Your brothers were going to East Chop to go climb on the rocks and they saw that evil thing in his yard with Chip in his mouth. He just grabbed my poor little puppy in his teeth and shook him until he was dead. My poor little Chip!"

I try to remember if I had seen Chip when I left the house that morning and I can't. Then I do have to throw up and I cover my mouth and run for the bathroom. My mother comes after me and holds my hair while I get sick, rubbing my back and telling me I will be fine. After I am done, she helps me upstairs and tucks me in bed. She sits by my bed and rubs my head until I fall asleep.

I dream about Chip. My Indian village is all done and customers are there walking around. I am standing at the entrance and hundreds of people are coming in and throwing money at me. I am laughing and throwing the money in the air and catching it. I look up and see Chip running through my village. I am mad that he is running loose because he is knocking people over.

He runs over to me and jumps up, scratching at my legs, so I pick him up. I look up just in time to see why he wants me to hold him. It is so I can protect him.

Three giant huskies are running toward us. They have huge fangs and they are growling and barking.

I don't realize it at first, but even though they are dogs, they don't have doggie faces.

Their faces look just like Jim's, Pat's and Donny's.

Chapter 20

1983

On the first day back to school after vacation, I took the bus to the hospital. I went to my father's office but his secretary told me he was with the patient and had more waiting so he wouldn't be available until 5 o'clock.

I told her to just tell him that I came by and went outside and over to the small building next door to the hospital where my mother had her office.

Mom didn't have a secretary, just a little bell over the door that jingled when it was opened. The building used to be a house, so the first room off the front door used to be a living room but became Mom's waiting room. It was filled with women's magazines and toys for little kids.

Straight ahead there were two smaller rooms with doors that Mom said had been bedrooms but were now her office and her treatment room.

A doorway to the right led to what was the kitchen and was now a break room, where patients to the office could go in and make themselves a cup of coffee or tea.

Mom also always had a coffee cake, Danishes, or chocolate chip cookies on a platter for anybody who wanted a snack.

When I opened the door, Mom looked up from the papers on her desk that she was reading. When she saw that it was me, she pushed her reading glasses up on her head, came to me and gave me a big hug.

"Hi sweetie! Everything okay?"

I laughed, realizing that since I didn't usually come to her office her first reaction would be to think something was wrong.

"I'm fine, everything's fine. I just didn't feel like going home. Cabin fever, I guess. I finally got out after being there for a week and I didn't want to go back."

Now it was my mother's turn to laugh.

"That makes sense. Do you want a snack?"

I nodded and she led me into the break room. She put on a tea kettle and filled two cups with powdered cocoa. When the water was done she poured it into the cups and taking two spoons from the drawer, she mixed them. She brought them over to the table, gave one to me and put hers down in front of the other chair.

She grabbed a plate of cookies from the counter and peeling the plastic wrap away offered the plate to me. I took one, and she did too and then sat down across from me.

We sat in silence for a little while, drinking our cocoa and eating our cookies.

"How was school?"

She took a napkin from the napkin holder in the middle of the table and wiped her lips. I noticed with some amusement that it was the one I had made for her in shop class when I was in fifth grade.

"Not bad. I think even the teachers weren't too thrilled to be back, though. I did meet with the guidance counselor today."

"Excellent! What did you talk about?"

"She gave me some brochures for Tufts Veterinary School. I'm thinking that might be what I want to do."

I sipped my cocoa and then put it down and looked up at Mom when she didn't answer me. I was alarmed to see that there were tears filling her eyes.

She blinked and her tears spilled onto her cheeks, leaving a trail of mascara.

"Mom!" I said, alarmed. "What's the matter?"

"It's okay, honey. That's just what your brother always said he wanted to do. It just surprised me when you said it, that's all. I thought you wanted to go into psychology, or human medicine, like your father."

"I definitely thought about those things and I'm not totally sure right now. I haven't made a decision. I just think about Chip a lot. I always wished I could have helped him."

Mom took another napkin from the middle of the table and dabbed at her tear and mascara stained eyes and cheeks.

"No, Dora, you couldn't have done anything to help him. You were just a little girl, and you weren't even there"

I opened my mouth, about to tell her that I thought I had been there, when she pushed back her chair and stood up.

"Excuse me for just one minute."

She hurried out of the room and I heard the bathroom door close. She came back a few minutes later, with her hair redone and her make-up reapplied.

Nobody would ever have been able to guess that she had just been crying. Even her voice, when she spoke, was calm and steady.

"So, where were we? What happened to you following in my footsteps? I thought that maybe someday you would take over this practice."

"Nah, probably not. How did you even end up working here, anyway?" I asked.

"There were some situations going on at home when you were little, with your brother, before, and then after he, you know, so we took you off-Island to see a doctor. Just to make sure you were okay, not traumatized. Do you remember?"

"No. Not really."

"I just got to talking with the doctor, mentioned that I had been a psychiatric nurse and how there was very little here on the Island to help people with psychiatric issues. So, we opened up the office and I started working here. You were like ten, maybe eleven years old. I had been home with all of you kids since Jim was born. I decided it was time to get myself back into the workplace."

"Oh. I thought you always worked here, like my whole life. But, yeah, I remember now when you started working here."

1977

My mom starts working at the hospital after Tommy dies. I know my father is happy that she is making her own money.

Most days when I get home from school, my mother is already home and she sends me upstairs or outside to play so she can rest.

But there are some days that she doesn't come home before me; that she has to work late.

When this happens, she has Olivia's mother babysit for me and I walk home with Olivia to her house. These are my favorite days. Olivia and I play and then my mother picks me up and we go home to have dinner.

On the days that my mother is home, I am pretty bored, playing by myself. My brothers usually have practice for one sport or another or are at their friends' houses.

I am not allowed to bother my mother between 4 and 5 because she says she needs to re-energize after a hard day at work.

The worst days are the ones when my mother gets stuck at work and my brothers come home to watch me. It is okay when they all come home. We go down cellar and play until my mother comes home and calls us for dinner.

There is a couch in the cellar near the pool table. My brother says that he has a new fun game for us to play. I want to tell him I already play this game with Jim and I don't like it all.

Nobody else is home; he is the only one who comes home. He says I have to take off my clothes and lay down on the couch.

"It's fun," he says. "I promise. Don't cry, everything will be fine."

I do cry and what he told me is a lie. It is not fun and everything is not alright.

Chapter 21

1983

The week after Dad moved into the new house, Mom went off-Island to go shopping with her friends. Olivia came over to hang out.

I finally decided that I had to talk to someone about what I remembered or I was going to burst.

"Hey, Olivia," I said while we were sitting around in front of the TV. "Remember I asked you if you remembered a lot about being a kid?"

"I don't know," she said.

"Well, what I really wanted to ask you if you ever, like, heard a song or something and it made you remember something from when you were a kid?"

"I don't think so. Why?" she asked.

I told her about being at Stacy's and hearing the song. I left out the part about the LSD though. Then I told her about my partial memory.

"Yeah, so what?" She asked when I finished. "If I recall correctly your brothers were loud-mouths. They were probably arguing over a football game."

"Then why would they freak out about me seeing them?"

"I don't know, Dora. Maybe they were smoking pot and they were fighting about who was hogging the joint. They wouldn't want you to see that."

"I don't think so. That doesn't feel right. And Tommy was dead the next day."

"You're sure about that? It was the next day? You don't sound so sure."

"No, I guess I'm not sure."

"Memories are really weird like that. You take what you remember and mesh it all up together. It probably just seems like they happened at the same time, cause they're two major things you remember. Forget about it. I'm sure it's nothing."

"You're probably right, but I have to know for sure. Can you do me a favor?"

Olivia sighed deeply and turned her attention away from the television to me, for the first time since we started talking.

"What?"

"The real estate agent is having an open house today. I need someone to go with me and keep her busy so I can go up to the attic for a minute."

"You're gonna drive me batty, Dora."

"Please, Olive Oyl?" I begged, resorting to using her pet name, knowing she couldn't deny me.

"Fine, I'll go with you. Then you'll forget about it?"

"Hopefully," I said.

We walked over to the house and fortunately when we got there, there were a bunch of cars parked out front, so Olivia and I could just blend in with everyone else there.

I had Olivia wear one of Mom's pantsuits so she would look like an adult. She put her hair up in a bun and wore some of Mom's dangling earrings. We didn't want to look like a couple of kids going into the open house. When we went inside the real estate agent came over and looked at us kind of funny.

I didn't realize until then what an actress Olivia was.

"Hello, I'm Marla Caldren and this is my daughter, Agnus. My husband asked me to come and take a peek at the house. He had to work today."

"Your daughter?" the agent asked. "You look so young."

Olivia leaned over and spoke in a stage whisper, "She's actually my step-daughter. The poor dear just lost her own mother recently to a tragic car accident. I don't put any emphasis on the 'step'."

"Oh, I'm so sorry," the agent said. "You can take a look around if you'd like. There is coffee and pastries in the kitchen. I'll be right here if you have any questions."

"Thank you, dear."

I thought Olivia was putting it on a little thick, but the agent seemed to buy it. Olivia and I went into Mom's special room.

I leaned over to Olivia and whispered, "Jeez, the least you could have done was give me a good name."

Olivia ignored me and walked to the middle of the room then spun around.

"Oh, darling, isn't this just a precious room? I think my parlor furniture would be just perfect in here!"

"Shut up, Olivia," I mumbled under my breath, trying my hardest not to just burst out laughing.

We quickly walked around through the bottom floor and then I told Olivia to go and ask about the neighborhood and the schools and stuff and I snuck up the stairs.

There were a few people walking around upstairs, but I was able to scoot by them unnoticed and go up the attic stairs.

When I got to the top of the stairs, I was breathing so heavy I had to sit down on a step so that I didn't pass out. I didn't think it was the heat or the dust up there that took my breath away, but it didn't help.

After a minute I got up and started back up the stairs. I stopped at the second to the top step, sure if I took that next step, I was going to trip and fall. I wasn't really sure where that thought was coming from, so I grabbed the rail and took a big, exaggerated step to clear the stair.

The attic was mostly cleaned out, but the bureau was still there, and behind it, my dollhouse decorating materials.

Everything was the way I had left it: clumps of glue-hardened tissues, my scissors, the roll of wallpaper. I didn't go over to it though. I went to the window, opened it and climbed out onto the porch roof.

I wasn't brave like my brothers, who just walked around on the roof like they were walking on the ground. I put one foot out on the roof and kept the other inside, while I took several deep breaths and exhaled slowly. Finally, I got enough nerve and swung my other leg out.

I knew exactly what I was looking for and was hoping that I didn't find it. If I didn't, then I could do what Olivia said and just forget the whole thing. If I did, I wasn't sure what I would do.

I stood there and grasped the window frame, unfortunately for me, right where there was a nail sticking out. I pulled my hand away, but it was too late.

My palm had a two inch long cut in it, because I dragged my hand across the nail, instead of just lifting it up, because I was more afraid of falling off the roof, than I was of a nail. It didn't matter, though, I had already seen it - a faded rusty stain on the flat part of the roof, that I knew had once been bright red, surrounded by several perfectly round indentations.

I walked back along the edge of the wall and climbed in the window. I sat on the floor underneath it and opened up my backpack. I found an old napkin and pushed it against my hand to stop the bleeding, willing myself not to cry.

There was one more thing I needed to check and then I had to get out of there and away from Olivia. There was no way I was going to let anyone see me crying.

In the far corner of the attic, there was a loose board. My brothers used to hide their cigarettes and stuff in there to get before they went out on the roof. I had no idea if I would find anything in there, and I already had the confirmation that I needed.

Something had happened on that roof and I had seen it. I went over to the board and put my foot on the edge, the way I had seen my brothers do a million times when I was spying on them and pushed down a little bit. The board popped up exactly the way it had done for them all those times.

I grabbed it and tossed it aside then dropped to my knees in front of the hole. I pushed aside some insulation that was tucked in the slot, and there it was, just like I knew it would be: a metal pole.

I lifted it up and held it in my hands. It was about a foot long and one end came to a point that was exactly the same size as the indentations in the shingles. It was a piece of the old antenna that was on the house from before there was cable.

I sat on the floor and scooted back in the corner. I ran my hands across the pole. It was clean, but I knew it had been washed. The moment I dreaded for so long was finally there.

My partial memory came back to me, this time complete and as real and vivid to me right then, it was as though it was happening all over again.

1976

When I go to bed that night, I wear my flannel Lanz of Salsburg nightie because it is cold out and my nightie is warm and cozy. I fall asleep snuggled into my blankets, toasty and comfy.

Sometime later I hear my name being shouted. I think somebody is calling me. I quickly get out of bed and rush into the hallway. I don't take the time to put on my slippers or my bathrobe because the voice calling my name sounds urgent.

As I round the corner, I realize the voices are coming from the roof. I climb the set of stairs that lead into the attic.

At the far end of the attic there is a window that looks out onto the roof over the porch. It is behind the house, so my brothers went out there all the time to hang out, and nobody could see them.

I realize as I stand there that they are not yelling at me. They're yelling but it's about me.

From where I stand I can see Pat. He is banging something against the roof and I can't tell what it is until he pulls it toward him. It is my brother Tommy. Both Jim and Donny are standing off to the side of him, and Jim's hands are behind his back.

"Did you?" Pat screams in Tommy's face. "Did you rape Dora?"

"I already told you! I swear to God, I never raped anyone!"

"So help me, if I find out that you ever touched Dora, I will fucking kill you!" Pat slams him against the roof again and the whole house shakes.

Tommy struggles to get loose, but he is no match for his big brother.

"I never touched Dora. Why won't you listen to me?"

"Why should we believe you? You raped that other girl! A 12 year-old, for Christ's sake! Why not Dora?" Jim yells.

"I did not rape that girl and you know it! You know what really happened!"

"Yeah, except you're the only one who says it!" Donny chirps in.

"It's the truth!" Tommy proclaims. "And what does that have to do with Dora, anyway? She's a little kid! My little sister! I would never do anything to hurt her!"

"Well, somebody did! I know it! I can tell by looking in her eyes!" Pat shouts.

"If you want to know the answer to that question, maybe you should ask Ji…."

And then I see it. Something that nobody should ever see.

My brother Jim brings his hand from behind his back. In it is a piece of the antenna from the roof and he shouts, "Watch out, Pat!" as he lunges toward where Tommy is being held down on his back.

I hear the metal strike the roof and see Tommy as he jerked out of the way.

"What the hell are you doing? You're going to kill me! This isn't even funny! Let me go!" Tommy screams.

I see Jim swing the metal pole back again and then Pat lets Tommy go and jumps back. Tommy's feet and legs comes to where I can see them, as his body slides down the side of the roof.

His legs jerk a couple of times and then he lays still. As still as Piggily-Wiggily.

"What the hell did you do?" Pat screams.

"I didn't mean to!" Jim yells back. "I was just trying to scare him! He moved!"

Donny stands up from where he had been hunched down next to Tommy. "Guys, I think he's dead…."

"What are we gonna do?" Pat howls, pacing around.

"Shut up! I'll figure something out! Just shut up!"

"Ma and Dad are gonna kill us!"

"We'll bring him across the street, say he did it to himself," Jim suggests.

"What, stabbed himself in the head with a pole?" Pat asks incredulously.

"No, we'll have to shoot him, leave him the gun, write a note about how he was too guilty to go on living."

"What? No, we can't do that!" Pat protests.

"So, you're going to have us go to jail for killing him?"

It was then that Donny glances over and notices me standing in the attic.

"Dora!" he shouts, not to me, but to Jim and Pat.

Jim screams, "Get her the fuck out of here!"

Donny scrambles in through the window and grabs me, putting his hands over my eyes and dragging me down the stairs and through the hallway, back into my bedroom, where he pushes me onto my bed.

"What did you see? Did you see anything?" Donny screams in my face.

"Nothing," I scream back. "I didn't see nothing."

Chapter 22

1983

Jim decided that he wanted to be like Dad, so he ran for selectman in Oak Bluffs. Dad had quit when Tommy died and just worked at the hospital. Jim had gotten his degree in Political Science so it was pretty obvious that he had planned to go into politics when he started college.

Dad had been a good selectman. It was his idea to start the annual August fireworks in town. I remember him talking to mother about it before he even discussed it with the other selectman.

He told my mother that he thought it would be a nice thing to do, to thank the summer people for coming to the Island and leaving their money behind when they left, and for the Islanders to celebrate the fact that they were leaving. They both laughed for a while about that. Dad talked to the other selectman, and the next year they had the first fireworks show, but they said it was to thank the tourists for visiting.

Jim won his election by what Dad said was "a landslide" and Dad and Jim started hanging out, talking about politics.

I stopped going to visit my father all together because the odds of Jim being around were pretty good. I didn't even bother with excuses anymore. I just said that I didn't want to go.

I overheard Mom talking to Dad on the phone about it and she said that was just how teenage girls were and that I would come around eventually and want to visit him.

Dad must have said something about "silly girl things" because Mom started to tease me about that whenever I was "in a mood," as she liked to say.

Them thinking that I was going through some kind of stage and was just going to all of sudden decide I wanted to go visit wasn't very likely, but they could think that all they wanted. It kept me from having to explain anything.

1976

Spying on my brothers has become one of my favorite past-times. On the day before Tommy's funeral, I hear them go out on the roof, so I sneak up the stairs and crawl under the railing to get behind the bureau.

Everybody in my house is sad and talks in quiet voices all the time.. Even my brothers who are usually loud and laughing and horsing around all the time, walk around with their heads down and are quiet.

Since Jim came and picked me up at school and Donny told me Tommy was dead, we hadn't been back to school, but it wasn't fun like a vacation or a weekend. It is so sad I actually want to go to school.

I have to listen really hard to hear them.

Pat says, "I'm wicked worried. You think they bought it all, the note and everything? That he really killed himself?"

"Why wouldn't they? It was typed on his typewriter. Mom said it was his signature, and he admitted to raping that girl and feeling guilty about it. Why wouldn't they buy it?" Jim asks.

"I don't know, I'm just nervous someone will get suspicious," Pat says.

"Well, you shouldn't be. It's gonna be fine," Jim replies.

"Yeah? How do you know? What if they have guys like on that show Quincy Ma watches, and they figure it out?" Pat asks.

"First of all, they don't have anything like that here.. That's not even real. Nobody is gonna figure anything out. His head blew up like a watermelon. There is, like no way anyone will figure out what really happened"

"What if they do?" Donny asks.

149

"Listen, Tommy was about to go to court for rape. It made total sense that he woulda' killed himself. Nobody is even gonna question that. They're not even gonna look."

"Yeah, but just say they do. Maybe some guy here watches those Quincy and checks just so he can be a hero like them," Pat says.

"You guys totally don't get it, do you? Martha's Vineyard is like a perfect place. They would never try to look for something else. It would destroy the fairy tale image. A suicide is bad enough. The cops'll all look at it as a good riddance. No trial. Nothing. It's over and that's it. Besides, with Dad being Selectman and all, he won't want any big investigation."

"We're going to hell," Pat says.

"No, we aren't," Jim replies. "It was an accident. It's not like it was on purpose. You need to just forget all about it. He killed himself. That's the story, and we're sticking to it."

Chapter 23

1983

The Friday before Easter Jim invited us all to a fancy restaurant in Edgartown. It was obvious to me that he had some big announcement. Maybe Maria was pregnant and they were going to have to move up the wedding, which wasn't scheduled until the early fall. Mom would be so mad.

Maybe he found out Maria was cheating on him and the wedding was off. It didn't really matter to me what his announcement was, as long as it was bad. I wasn't wishing for anything good to happen to any of my brothers.

The Country Club restaurant was pretty fancy, so Mom and I got dressed up. I wore the dress Mom bought me for my date with Jared.

I had worked at a hotel next door in housekeeping the summer before and planned on going back the next year. It was a pretty good job. It paid a lot of money and I got a ton of babysitting jobs out of it, too. Tourists who stayed there were pretty desperate to go out without their kids and I could easily make a couple few hundred dollars a night.

When we got to the restaurant and the hostess brought us to the table, Jim and Maria were already there. So much for my idea that the wedding wasn't going to happen.

Dad and Donny had to get Pat off the 5:15 boat in Vineyard Haven so we only ordered our drinks. We were going to wait until they got there to order our food.

Mom and Maria talked about wedding plans and Jim tried to talk to me about school and stuff. I kept myself focused on the ice cubes in my drink that I was pushing down with my straw, trying to make them stay on the bottom of the glass, and just answered his questions with single syllables.

I was ecstatic when Dad got there, because Jim stopped talking to me and all the guys started discussing sports and school.

When the waitress brought over the menus Jim said, "It's my treat, Dora. Order whatever you want."

I scanned the menu for a puke bucket because I was pretty much what I felt like I needed every time Jim opened his mouth.

"I'll have the boiled twin lobsters," I said to the waitress when she came back to take our order because number one: it was the most expensive thing on the menu and number two: there wasn't much to eat in a lobster, and I really didn't feel like eating at all.

"There you go, Dora," Jim said laughing. "That's what I'm talking about."

Laugh now, Jimmy- Boy, I thought, because you won't be laughing as soon as I make my announcement, the one that I had decided to make to come clean about my memories.

All of them.

Since Olivia and I had gone to the open house I had been struggling with how to handle what I knew. I thought about going to the cops, after all I had physical proof right on my top shelf in the closet under a pile of sweaters I didn't wear anymore.

But then I worried about what would happen. Would they lose the piece of the antenna? Tell my parents that I had lost my mind and that they should send me to Taunton? Going to Taunton was an expression that meant "going crazy," but it was also literal because of the mental institution there.

I worried about these things, because like Jim had said all those years ago, how far would the police go to protect the fairy tale image of Martha's Vineyard? They had found a guy hanging from a tree on Edgartown/Vineyard Haven

Road awhile back and called it a suicide even though everyone knew he was the biggest drug-dealing rip-off artist who had about a million people who wanted to kill him.

Besides, everyone said that the way he was hanging, there was no way he could have done it to himself. So, I decided the only way I could do it was to tell my parents and my brothers everything I knew and then go to the police. There was no way they could cover it up then.

I decided I was going to make my announcement right after Jim made his, whatever it was. It became obvious that he was in no rush, though. After a few minutes of small talk, the waitress brought our food and we ate our dinner.

After we were done and the waitress cleared away our plates and took our dessert order, Jim cleared his throat and pushed his chair back a couple of inches. It was time for his big announcement.

"So, I asked all of you here tonight because I have some exciting news I wanted to share with you."

"What is it already?" Mom asked. "I've been sitting here all night barely able to contain myself!"

"I've enjoyed my time as Selectman so much that I've decided to run for State Rep. I already have all my signatures and I'm going to be interviewing potential campaign managers in the next few weeks. From there I plan on running for Governor of Massachusetts, and after that, well who knows, maybe the White House."

Everyone at our table was totally frozen. It was weird. It was like we were the audience at a particularly riveting ballet and the waitresses and the other diners were the performers, except we were all staring at Jim.

Mom was the first one to thaw out. She clamped both hands over her mouth and tears sprang from her eyes. She jumped from her chair and ran over to Jim and hugged him.

"Oh, Jim, I am so proud of you!"

Dad stayed in his chair, but he was beaming. I swore I could see rays of light coming out of his ears and his nose. He reached across the table and shook Jim's hand.

"Congratulations, son. I have no doubt you'll achieve all your goals."

I glanced around the table at my family. Maria rested her head on Jim's shoulder and wrapped her arms around his neck. Her sleeve moved a little and I saw she was wearing a bracelet that said, "Future First Lady."

The sad thing was, I could picture her as a First Lady and I could picture Jim as President someday, too.

Pat had been observed at his last basketball game by NBA scouts and Donny had gotten his acceptance letter from Southeastern University, where he would be going to study Pre-Law, his first step to becoming Attorney General, which would be even easier for him if his brother was Governor. It was the perfect time for my announcement:

"I have an announcement, too," I said. "Mom, Dad, I know you have gone all these years thinking that Tommy killed himself, but it's not true. His brothers killed him and I saw them do it."

My mother's eyes went big and round.

She looks at each of my brothers in turn, "Is that true? Is what Dora said the truth? Did you kill Tommy?"

My brothers all started talking at once.

"She's lying because she is jealous that I am running for State Rep.!"

"She had a nightmare, that's all, a nightmare!"

"She's crazy! She needs to go to Taunton!"

Then I said, "I found the piece of antennae that Jim used to stab him in the eye. Then they shot him in the head and arranged him with the gun in his hands. They shot him, so nobody would see the stab wound and it would look like he did it himself."

"Why would we stab our own brother? That makes no sense, Dora," Jim said.

Dad asked, "Dora, why are you saying all this?"

"Because it's the truth! I can't live with knowing this secret anymore!"

"Are you sure it's the truth? You're not just trying to get your brothers in trouble are you? These are very serious accusations," my father said.

"Is this some kind of sick joke, Dora? Because I don't think it's very funny!" Mom said.

"I am telling the truth. They did it to cover up the fact that Jim was molesting me."

"Dora! How could you?" Jim asked, at first seemingly shocked by what I had said, but then breaking down. "I mean, how did you? How did you remember? You were supposed to forget all about it! Think you were having a bad dream! I had it planned out so carefully. How did you remember?"

"Well, Jim, it turns out my attention span is a little better than a gnat's."

Dad was already behind the bar using their phone to call the police. My brothers get up and try to run out of the restaurant, but other people grab them and hold them until the police came.

Chapter 24

1983

When I woke up the next morning, I was disgusted with myself. The way I planned out my announcement and the aftermath in my head was perfect, but of course I chickened out and didn't actually do it.

The logic I used to not make the announcement was this: My parents had three sons who were doing things that would make any parent proud. They had one son who had been a source of colossal embarrassment, and he had been gone for eight years.

With one sentence I would change all that. They would have one son who would become a martyr, a diversion to cover up what their other sons did. They would have three sons who would be murderers, and one of them the mastermind behind making it look like a suicide.

Their sons would be convicted and go to jail, and their other son still wouldn't come back. They would be left with one child, a daughter, who they could potentially hate for destroying everything they had believed all those years.

With that one sentence, I would ruin my parents' lives, as surely as Jim, Pat, and Donny had ruined Tommy's. Every dream, every potential for success that my brothers had, would be over.

Could I even trust my own memory enough to do that? What if I was wrong? What if the hole in the shingle and the hidden antenna pole were all just coincidences? Maybe Olivia was right. Maybe I had just meshed a couple of memories. How could I ever be sure enough to do that to my parents?

The other thing I was worried about was the way my parents always seemed to believe my brothers over me. I asked myself, if I was my mother or father would I believe me? My brothers had all grown up and were well on their way to being successful; the stories I had to tell seemed unbelievable, far-fetched even.

And there was always the fact that I wasn't so sure I believed them myself. Would I be convincing and confident when I shared my memories, or would my own self-doubt come through and make it seem like I was making everything up?

I walked around the whole weekend in a fog. Every memory I had, that came to me slowly over the year, bombarded my thoughts all weekend long. I was thrilled when Monday rolled around and I could get back to school. After school I had an Honor Society meeting. All day long there had been a rumor about something important that was going to be discussed and the principal said over the loud speaker that all Honor Society members should make sure they attended the meeting.

By the time Mrs. DeBettencourt, the Honor Society advisor, got to the meeting, we were all so excited nobody could sit still. It took Mrs. D. like ten minutes to get everyone settled down.

"I know that you're all aware of the new policy they put in place, that you have to be a junior or a senior to go to the prom," Mrs. D. said.

"It's so unfair!" Missy, who was a sophomore, said. "My boyfriend is a junior and I can't even go with him."

"I know, it does seem unfair, but one of your classmates has petitioned the principal for a compromise, and he agreed to let the freshman and sophomore classes have a formal dance, as well," Mrs. D. said.

"That's pissa!" Adrianna said.

"Please don't use that word," Mrs. D said.

"Why not? It's not a swear."

"It might not be an official swear, but it's not a very nice sounding word and it doesn't fit coming out of the mouth of a beautiful young lady like yourself."

Mrs. D. was right. "Pissa" and "wicked pissa" were words we used to describe something when it was cool, but I didn't think it seemed like a nice word either, even though I used it myself all the time.

"So, what does everyone else think? Because there are a couple of catches. First, the dance would have to be held here in the gymnasium and the principal has asked that you, as a club, organize the whole thing. It will be quite a bit of work. You will be responsible for planning it, decorating, and cleaning up," Mrs. D. said.

"We can definitely do it!" Olivia said.

Everyone started talking at once – about what to call it, what theme we should have, where we could get decorations and what we would do about music.

"Alright, settle down, kids. I guess I'll take that as a yes, but you're going to have to sit down and have an orderly discussion. There is a lot of planning to do and not much time."

Everyone moved their desks in a circle and Olivia, who was the secretary, took out a pad of paper to take notes.

"Does everyone agree that we'll call it 'The Spring Fling'?" Olivia asked.

Everyone did agree, so Olivia wrote it on the top of her page in big, flourishing letters.

"Who was the kid that asked the principal about doing this?" a kid named Jonas asked.

"Stacy something, um, let me see," Mrs. D. checked her notes. "Stacy Cullen."

"Humph," a girl named Linda said. "Why would she do that? She's a loser. She's in my lit class and she ditches like every other day."

"Maybe she's turning over a new leaf. She suggested that the Honor Society run the dance and offered to help." Mrs. D said.

"How is she going to help?" I asked. I had a bad feeling.

"She wants to work with the Yearbook Committee to gather pictures and she joined the Photography Club, so that she can make a slideshow highlighting the freshman and sophomore classes' achievements."

My fellow Honor Society members all voiced their opinions that they thought it was a cool idea and that Stacy must have been really trying to change, since she offered to do such a nice thing.

I knew better, though. Stacy would never change and she never did anything to be nice. I would have to stay alert and pay attention to what Stacy was doing so that I wouldn't get caught off guard, like I did at Joe's party.

We couldn't plan the dance for the same weekend as the junior prom because there wouldn't be enough chaperones for both dances at the same time, so we chose the weekend after.

There were a few good ideas for a theme, but I was happy they chose mine – a Monet garden. We made hundreds of flowers out of tissue paper and painted murals to hang on the walls. We decided to hire a D.J. after a lot of discussion about hiring one of the bands that kids at our school were trying to start. That idea ended up getting rejected when we found out that even the best of them could only play three songs.

The dance was another welcome distraction for me. I stayed after school every day to make flowers and I offered to be in charge of organizing the refreshments, which took up a lot of my time. Jim had already put up some campaign signs around town. Everywhere I went, I couldn't get away from him.

The weekend of the prom Mom and I went to New Bedford to stay with her friend and go shopping for a dress for me. Mom was happy because all the stores had formal dresses on sale because prom season was pretty much over.

Jared had asked me to the dance and he went away that weekend, too. He went to Falmouth with his mother to get his tuxedo. It seemed silly to me that we were going to wear gowns and tuxedos in our school gym, but our decorations were pretty spectacular, so I figured it wouldn't be recognizable.

We even made posters to cover the basketball championship banners, which was good for me since most of them were from years that my brothers were on the team.

Mom took me to her hairdresser again and then we went to the new house so I could get dressed, even though we weren't living there; it would be a couple weeks before we moved in.

Dad had put up an arbor at the end of the walkway and planted rose bushes all across the front yard, like a fence made out of flowers. Mom wanted to take pictures of Jared and me with them in the background.

When Jared got there to pick me up, Mom drove me absolutely nuts. Jared came to the door and knocked, so I answered it. Then Mom came running in and made Jared get back in his car so she could take a picture of him "pulling up and getting out of his car."

Then she staged a picture of me coming down the stairs, with Jared standing in the doorway.

It took Jared ten minutes to get the right look on his face: awed by my beauty, Mom had told him. She took a picture of him showing me the corsage, and I had to look surprised at its beauty. Then she took pictures of him pinning it on me.

We finally got outside for about a hundred pictures under the arbor and in front of the roses. Then she took pictures of us getting in the car. I swear she was still taking pictures of the dust we left behind after we were gone.

I wasn't on the set-up committee so when Jared and I got to the dance, it was the first time I saw the gym decorated. It looked even better than I imagined. It was like stepping into one of Monet's paintings. The D.J. was pretty good. He played some good music and everyone got up to dance. I had obviously done a good job of organizing the refreshments because everyone was eating and saying how good everything was.

With everything I had to do to get ready in the weeks leading up to the dance, I kind of forgot about Stacy and her slide show. When the D.J. came over his speaker and said that the slideshow was about to begin, my heart skipped a beat. They dimmed the lights and everyone started cheering.

The D.J. put on a song about "memories" and a picture of our freshman orientation flashed on the screen. As the show continued there was a bunch of pictures of kids in class, in the cafeteria, on the boat heading to away games. I started to relax and enjoy it. I had thought the worst of Stacy, but maybe everyone was right, maybe she was trying to change.

She certainly was doing a good job for the photography club. They didn't usually make slide shows, and Stacy had to learn how to use a pretty complicated program and had to teach everyone else.

The next part was pictures of everyone when they were little. A funny baby picture came up on the screen and everyone started to laugh.

Someone behind me yelled, "Right here! That's Joey!" I looked back at Joey and laughed, too.

Then I realized I was the only one laughing. I turned around slowly and looked up at the screen. The slide had changed and there wasn't a picture up there on the screen.

There was a written message: "How well do you know your classmate, Dora Culligan? This is her brother, in case you didn't know."

The next ten slides were all newspaper headlines from the Gazette, with a couple pictures of Tommy in handcuffs, for good measure; pictures that were never even published in the newspaper. The headlines were:

Local Teen Arrested for Rape of a Child

Child Victim of Rape to Testify in Closed Chambers

D.A. Seeks Maximum Sentence for Teenage Rapist

Rapist out on Bail: Awaits Trial

Thomas Culligan, Oak Bluffs Teen, Commits Suicide.

I get up and run. From the auditorium. From the school. I run across the street and into the woods. I lose my shoes in a mud puddle. I don't care. I don't care. I have to run. I have to get away, I scream. My face is on fire. I am so embarrassed. I don't know where to go. I don't know what to do.

I am thinking of "Carrie." I am covered with proverbial pig's blood. I wish I had her powers. I wish I could go back and kill Stacy Cullen with my mind. I stop when I step on something sharp and it bites into my foot.

I sit on the ground. It is wet. I am going to ruin my gown. I don't care! I DON'T CARE! I scream as loud as I can. I sob. I lay on the ground, in the mud, holding my hurt foot and crying until I lose my voice. I hate my parents. I hate their guts.

Why couldn't they have moved away from this horrible Island after Tommy died? Then nobody would have known. I wouldn't have met Stacy and taken her fucking LSD and had that original memory.

I probably never would have remembered what I had. I may have heard the song somewhere else and remembered standing in the attic, but that would have been it! I never would have gone into my old room again.

I would have never gone into the attic. I would never have remembered all of the horrible things. I would have never met Stacy and she never would have planned this slideshow to embarrass me. None of my friends knew what happened to my brother, what he supposedly did. We were all too little. Now they all know.

Because of Stacy. How did she get those headlines? How did she get those pictures? If we lived off Island nobody would have even known anything. Stacy must have heard that I had a brother who had died and searched old newspapers to discover what happened. The information she found was probably better than she expected.

How will I ever show my face in school again? How could my parents ever have shown their faces again? Did their other three sons make up for what everyone thought about their other son? Everyone thought they were so perfect.

Then and now. I decide right then and there that I won't let this go on anymore.

I have to tell. When I get home, if Mom is there, I will tell her everything. If she isn't, I plan to wait up for her and tell her then.

I have to clear my brother's name.

Chapter 25

1983

I finally decided I better get up and go home before Mom got back from going out with Dad. I walked through the woods and the back roads to get there.

When I got home the answering machine was blinking with 29 calls. I checked the first few.

They were all from Olivia and Jared. I erased them and then went to take a shower. I got as much mud as I could off the gown and hid it in my closet. When I checked the answering machine again, there were already a couple more calls from Jared.

I had no choice but to call him back. I didn't want him calling my mother and telling her what happened, because that's what he said he was going to have to do, because he was so worried about me.

"Dora?" he answered on the first ring.

"It's me."

"Where are you? I drove around all over the place looking for you. Are you alright?"

"I'm home. I'm fine."

"I can't believe that Stacy Cullen, if she was a guy, I would'a…"

"Jared, I don't even want to talk about it. I just called to tell you I was alright so you would stop calling, okay?"

"But…"

"I have to go. I'll call you tomorrow. Bye."

I hung up before he could say anything else, then I called Olivia. She had something a little more interesting to tell me.

"I'm not sure who or how, but after you left the ambulance had to come for Stacy."

"Are you serious?"

"Totally. You can't let this bother you. Nobody cares. It happened a long time ago, and it had nothing to do with you. If anything, Stacy just made herself look like a jerk. I must have heard twenty people say they wanted to kill her for doing that to you. So, promise me, okay? You'll forget about it."

"I promise, Olive Oyl. Thanks for telling me that."

"It's the truth, so you don't have to thank me. I can't wait for Monday to see Stacy. I heard she was bleeding like a stuck pig!"

I got into bed before Mom came home and pretended I was asleep when she came in my room. She shook me gently.

"Dora, you're home so early! Didn't you have a good time?"

"I did. It was awesome. I was just tired, so Jared and I left a little early."

"Good, I'm glad I caught you before you fell asleep. Let's get your medicine going."

She left the room and came back with the small bottle of clear liquid and a needle, things that were so familiar to me and so much a part of my daily routine, that I didn't even think about it. I had actually forgotten how freaked out Stacy, Brandy, and Laurie were about the shots.

My mother prepared the needle and then held it up to squeeze a little bit of fluid out to ensure there were no air bubbles. She lifted my blanket and reached for my foot. I pulled it away.

"Dora, come on, I need to go to bed."

"Why don't you put it in my arm, like normal?"

"We've been through this before. Do you really need me to explain it again?"

I let her grab my foot, "I guess not."

She spread my pinky toe away and injected the medicine in.

"There you go," she straightened the blankets, put the needle and bottle on my nightstand and then sat on the edge of my bed.

I really wanted her to just leave so I could fume about what happened, but she tucked the blankets up around my neck and rubbed my back. She started talking, but her voice was distant and lulling, and although I couldn't tell what she was saying, I was comforted by it.

After a couple of minutes, I felt like I was floating and her voice went on and on while she continued to rub my back, smooth back my hair, and adjust my blankets. This was what we did every night, and honestly that night I really needed it.

The next thing I knew it was morning and I was alone in my room. Now that I had time to think, I decided that I had two options at this point. I had already tried to make the decision on two different occasions to tell what I know and have wimped out both times.

If I couldn't get up the nerve to tell, then I was just going to have to live with what I knew. I could try to forget about it, I did it once, maybe I could do it again. Everyone could just continue with their lives, believing what they always had.

My brothers would go on and do great things. They would have successfully and literally gotten away with murder. I would be the only one who would ever know the truth, and if I didn't tell it would be like it never even happened.

Could I accept the fact that it was an accident, like Jim claimed it was? That making it look like Tommy killed himself was the best thing for everybody?

Wasn't it true that if they hadn't killed him, my parents would have been forced to sit through a trial and see their son convicted of rape?

He would still be in jail most likely and my mother would feel obligated to go on the boat every visiting day to go see him. How different my family would be today. I wasn't sure, but I bet having a brother in jail would have made my other brothers' lives turn out a lot different. I didn't know that they would be successful like they were now.

My brothers were sociopaths. That much was clear to me then. If I didn't tell and let them get away with murder, would I be an accessory? Would I be any better than they were? I remember being a little girl and hearing my parents talking about "right" and "wrong" and "gray areas".

I was in a gray area. I couldn't even figure out what was right. What if I decided not to tell and one of my brothers ever did anything like that again? I could tell myself that it was just an accident all I want, but then there's the thing with Chip, too.

I hated being that confused. I longed to be a little kid again, when things were simple and the biggest thing I had to worry about was whether or not there was a mouse in the basement. Well, I guess I did have a bit more to worry about back then, actually, but I didn't remember it, so it didn't really matter.

Chapter 26

1983

Jim's first fundraiser was held at the VFW. Mom and Dad sat together and held hands. I couldn't help but wonder if this whole reconciliation thing was for Jim's benefit. Keeping up appearances and all that.

Pat was there with a bunch of his college buddies and his fuck buddy girlfriend glued to his side. They hired some local band that was starting to make it big, on the Island anyway, and had a fancy dinner catered.

I pretty much tried to sit in the corner and be invisible. Much to my dismay, Pat's annoying girlfriend kept coming over and dragging me on to the dance floor. So much for being invisible.

I had been trying my hardest to figure out what the right thing to do was. Everything was too difficult, too confusing. No matter which of the scenarios I played in my head, the outcome was not going to be good.

The main problem was that my brothers had done something terribly wrong and they got away with it. I decided (again) that whatever happened, in order to live with myself, I was going to have to do the right thing, and that would begin with telling my parents.

If nobody believed me, or they sent me to Taunton, so be it. It would be the only way I could live in my own skin. Tommy was my hero, my protector, and now it was time for me to protect him.

On Monday after school I went home, fully determined to sit down with my mother and tell her, and then she and I could go together and tell Dad. When I got home, I was surprised at what I found.

I closed the door behind me and called out for my mother. She didn't answer, but that didn't surprise me, most days I beat her home. What was weird though was it felt like someone was in the house, but nobody answered when I called out.

I didn't put my backpack near the door like I usually did, but kept it slung over my back so I could swing it and hit any intruder I might discover in my kitchen.

By the time I tiptoed around the corner and had a full view of the kitchen where I could see who it was who was there, I had imagined and discarded about a thousand different scenarios, that ranged from the cable guy to a serial killer. Nothing prepared me for what I saw. Jim was leaning against the counter near the refrigerator.

His arms were crossed in front of his chest and he was shaking his head vehemently. Standing in front of him was Olivia. She had one hand on her hip and was waving the other one around as she talked to Jim.

I stopped and stared at them and Jim reached up and grabbed Olivia's hand. She stopped talking and turned around to look at me.

"Dora! You're finally home!" she said, which made no sense because I took the bus and came right to the house.

"What are you doing here?" I asked Olivia, even though there were a hundred more important questions I wanted to ask her like: how did you get here before the bus? And what are you talking to Jim about?

"I wanted to see if you wanted to hang out…"

She didn't sound very convincing and suddenly I was very, very suspicious.

"What's up with you, Jim? Why are you here?"

"Ma called and asked me to come by. She has to work late and she thought maybe you and I could go out and grab some dinner. After you do your homework, of course," Jim said.

"Uh huh. What were you guys talking about? It looked pretty intense," I said.

"Nothing, really. Just politics. Olivia doesn't one hundred percent agree with my platform," Jim winked at Olivia.

"Politics? Since when did you care about politics, Olivia?" I asked.

"I signed up for Civics next year. It's kinda interesting, I don't know," she stumbled over her words.

"Alright, Ms. Dora, get going on your homework and we'll go grab a pizza."

As suspicious as I had been up to that point, I shifted into full-fledged paranoia. I was convinced that I would not survive the trip out to dinner. Olivia told Jim what I suspected and although she did so innocently, she signed my death warrant.

Jim couldn't allow me to live with what I knew. Tomorrow they would find my body and probably a suicide note, that much I was sure about.

"I just remembered, Mrs. Jones asked me to babysit after school today. I've got to go." I turned to go back out the door.

What Jim said then made my blood turn to ice in my veins, because I didn't really have a babysitting job for Mrs. Jones.

"Don't worry about it. Mrs. Jones called and canceled."

"Oh, well that's fine then, because Mrs. Emerson wanted me to babysit and I told her I already was. So, I'll just go over there."

I didn't know anybody named Emerson, never mind babysat for them, but I doubted Jim knew that.

"Hold on, Dora!" Jim called. "At least let me give you a ride."

I realized then that Jim's car was not even parked in sight, which most likely meant he already had a plan for me and had to make sure nobody saw his car parked outside of our house.

When I got out the door, I didn't even look back for his car, I just ran. After a few minutes, when it got heavy, I realized I also didn't bother to put down my backpack.

I really didn't have a definitive plan about where I was going, I just went down the road. I heard a car coming, and sure that it had to be Jim, I jumped into a ditch on the side of the road. It was deep enough that I could do a drop roll and then turn around to look up just in time to see Jim drive past. Fortunately, he didn't see me.

I stayed in the ditch for a little while to make sure Jim had time to at least get out to the main road and also long enough to have Olivia show up if she had left my house and started walking down my street. When I was sure nobody was around, I climbed back up onto the road and started to run again.

Now, I had a destination. I was going to have to go to my father's house and tell him, no question about it. It was more than Tommy's reputation now. It was my life.

When I got to Dad's he wasn't home yet, so I hid behind a cluster of trees and tried to catch my breath. Jim pulled into the driveway about ten minutes after I got there and went up to the house where he knocked and tried looking in the windows. I lost my breath again, because I held it the whole time he was there.

If I thought I was just being paranoid before, this pretty much solidified the idea that Jim was looking to shut me up, because why would he be looking for me? I told him I was going to babysit, and I made up a person's name, so why would he be at Dad's looking for me?

Jim walked around to the back of the house, and Dad pulled into the driveway. I stood up, leaving my backpack behind the tree, to run to my father before Jim came back to the front.

I was too late, though, Jim came jogging around the side of the house and stopped right in front of my father, where he bent over, his hands on his knees, taking big gasping breaths, while he told my father something that I could not hear.

My father put his hands on Jim's shoulders and pulled him upright, and then keeping his hands where they were, he leaned close to Jim's ear and talked very quietly for a long time. The hair on the back of my neck stood up.

Dad let go of Jim and dropped his hands to his sides. Jim waved his arms around and said something back, very intensely, but quietly enough that I could not hear what he was saying. Dad said something back, shaking his finger at Jim and then Jim shook his head and covered his face with his hands.

My father reached over and grabbed Jim's hands, pulling them away from his face. Then my father started talking again and pointing one way up the road and then the other. Jim nodded, went back to his car, got in and drove away. My father stood there watching him for a minute and then he turned and walked toward the house.

I stayed behind the tree, frozen by my indecisiveness. What I just witnessed indicated to every fiber in my being that my father was involved in what had happened. There was no way that was possible though. A father could not have possibly had anything to do with the death of his own son, could he?

Standing behind the cluster of trees, I began to shake, it started at my feet and went all the way to the top of my head. I bent down and picked up my backpack, squeezing it to my chest in the hopes that it would help me stop shaking.

I stepped out from behind the tree as soon as my father closed the door behind him and on shaky legs moved as fast as I could toward the road.

I would go in the direction that Jim did not go and take as many shortcuts through the woods as I could make my way back to my mother's house. I couldn't have gotten five steps away from my hiding place when I heard my father's front door open and him shout, "Dora!"

He rushed to me and reached me just as my shaking legs grew too weak to support me any longer, and he caught me in his arms as my knees buckled.

My father led me into the house and over to the couch where he helped me sit down.

Then he muttered, "Hold on," and went into the kitchen.

He came back and handed me a box of tissue and a glass of water.

Then he opened his palm and held a pill out to me, "Here, take this, it will help you calm down. You are way too hyped up."

When I didn't reach for it, he said, "Come on, you wouldn't want me to call an ambulance now, would you? I'm getting a little worried here. If you don't calm down, I'm going to have to."

Since our hospital didn't have a crazy unit, and my father used the words "hyped up" and "ambulance," it was like he was reading my worst fears and threatening to send me to Taunton.

I reached out and took the pill and then swallowed it with a gulp of water. I figured whatever it was, taking it couldn't be worse than being sent away in an ambulance.

"Thank you," I said, gulping down some more water and then wiping the back of my hand across my lips.

"Dora, what's going on?" my father asked as he sat on the couch next to me.

"Nothing, Daddy. I just got scared. Jim scared me is all."

"Why? What could Jim have done to scare you?"

"I don't know. I'm just having silly girl things, like you say, that's it."

"Okay then. You rest here. I'm going to get you a wet face cloth to wash your face. Don't move."

He brought back a damp cloth and I wiped my face and hands. I hadn't realized how sweaty and dirty I was. He took the facecloth back from me and then fluffed the couch pillow, putting it against the arm of the couch. He helped me to lay down and then untied my shoes and took them off. I was starting to feel a little tired and laying down was a good thing.

My father left the room again and came back with a comforter from my room. As he walked toward me, I felt ashamed of myself.

How could I have ever thought my father would have anything to do with my brother's death? He was a good man, a good father, and he would do whatever he had to do to protect his children, not hurt them. He brought the comforter and tucked me in then he sat down and stroked my hair.

"Go back to sleep. You're having a bad dream."

1976

Jim catches me standing at the top of the stairs of the attic looking at him. I plan on running back down, but I am too late.

"Get her the fuck out of here!" Jim screams.
Donny climbs in the window and grabs me. He picks me up, one arm wrapped around my stomach and he covers my eyes with his other hand. Because he is not a whole lot taller than me, carrying me this way doesn't really work, and my legs thump on every step as we go down.

When we get to the bottom of the stairs he lets go of my eyes and grabs me under both of my shoulders, dragging me down the hallway and into my room. When we get to the doorway, he lets me go and I almost fall, but his hands are there, not to catch me, but to push me. I stumble forward toward my bed.

He is there before I can jump in and hide under my covers. He grabs me by my shoulders and screams in my face, so loud it hurts my ears and so close I can smell the potato chips he ate and I feel the spray of his spit across my face.

"What did you see? Did you see anything?"

He pushes me onto my bed. I scramble as far away from him as I can get and pull my pillow over my head.

"Nothing," I cry out. "I didn't see nothing!"

"You better tell me if you saw something or I'll punch you right in the kisser!"

"Donny!"

My father comes into my room and I am so happy to see him. I am afraid of what I saw and I am afraid of what Donny was going to do to me if he found out.

"Get back upstairs, your brothers have something to do, and they need your help."

When Donny doesn't move, my father points toward the door and shouts, "Now!"

Donny runs by him, ducking his head as if he thinks my father is going to hit him when he goes past.

My father comes over to my bed and holds my blankets up so I can climb underneath. After I do, he tucks the blankets in around my legs, then he rubs my hair and kisses me on the forehead.

"Are you okay, Princess?" I don't answer him and he smiles and kisses me again.

"You're fine, I promise, nothing is wrong, now go back to sleep. You're having a bad dream."

Chapter 27

1983

I stayed as still as I could on the couch and closed my eyes, pretending I was asleep. The only problem was I did feel like I was going to fall asleep, and I didn't want to. Now I had a definitive reason to be afraid of my father. I planned on waiting until he left the room and then I was going to run out the door and find my mother.

I heard a perfunctory knock on the front door and then it opened. When I turned my head to see who it was and saw Jim there, a scream grew in my throat till I felt like I was going to burst, but my throat seemed to have quit working.

"Hey, Sis," Jim said, sitting in the chair across from me.

My father came into my view and sat down on a chair across from Jim.

"What took you so long?"

"I went the way you said, I didn't see her, so I came right back. Somehow I knew she'd end up here anyway. Or did you find her walking up the road?"

"She was right outside, apparently hiding behind a tree the whole time we were talking."

"Did she hear us?"

"I doubt it, she was pretty far away, but regardless, knowing what she knows, hearing what we had to say isn't going to make any difference. We're going to have to take care of it either way. You want a beer?"

"Sure," Jim stood up.

"Grab one for me, too."

Jim left the room and I must have drifted off to sleep for a little while, because when I opened my eyes he was back taking his last sip of beer and opening another one.

"I know, it sucks."

"Well, at least she should sleep for a while. I gave her one of your mother's famous pills."

I must have faded out again, because I never heard Jim's answer. When I opened my eyes again, I was alone in the room, and I tried to kick off the blankets so I could go find my mother.

As with my voice before, my legs would not work. I tested other areas of my body like my arms and my head. Nothing would move. One part of my body that wasn't lacking in its ability to move was my heart. It was beating like crazy. My imagination was also not stalled.

For the first time the predicament I was in and its consequences played out fully in my mind's eye. My father and my brother, having no choice, would have to kill me.

Exactly what did I think, "We're going to have to take care of it either way" meant in the first place?

Ironically, they would probably make it look like a suicide. Since they had already done the gun thing, they would probably put me in the bathtub with a razor blade positioned between my unmovable fingers and slice me up until I would be sure to bleed out in the bathtub.

Then they would set out, typing a suicide letter and practicing my signature until it was good enough to add to the bottom of the note.

My mother would never have any idea that anything was amiss. She might go through her memories of the past few months and try to figure out if I had done or said anything that might have given her a clue about what I was planning to do.

My father and my brother, experts at this by now, would leave a trail of evidence that would leave no doubt in anybody's mind that I killed myself.

They would think my suicide was connected to my brother's and the funny thing was, they would be right, only it wouldn't connected in the way they thought.

In One Week:

"What a shame. She had so much potential. Why these kids do this kind of stuff, I'll never understand."

"Don't you remember her brother?"

"Not really. What about him?"

"He committed suicide a few years back."

"Interesting. There certainly must have been some sort of undetected mental illness running through the family. I mean, one kid could be a fluke, but two?"

"And, the craziest thing about it is that their mother is the liaison at the hospital for Taunton State. You'd think she'd know when her own family was in crisis. I don't know how we can trust her to recognize it in ours."

"It's still so sad that anybody would think there was something so bad in their lives that couldn't be fixed - that this was the only alternative. Such a waste."

Chapter 28

1983

The next time I opened my eyes, it was harder than ever, both my father and Jim were back in the living room, sitting down, but not talking.

If I could have moved, I would have jumped right up off the couch with excitement when the door opened and my mother burst in. I was saved.

"James? Jim?"

Mom rushed across the room and came to me. She sat on the end of the couch, adjusting my head so it was resting on her lap.

"What is going on? Why is she just laying here like she's paralyzed? What the hell did you do to her?"

"I just gave her one of your pills from the medicine cabinet. She was running around, all upset about something. Jim couldn't get her to tell him what it was."

"So, you thought it was a good idea to drug her up? Sometimes, James, for a highly educated man, you do some pretty stupid things."

I worked hard to hold on to consciousness, and had for the longest time so far, since I had taken the pill, but now I lost it. My eyes, so heavy, closed and the voices around me became an intermingled murmur.

How much later, I don't know, but I woke up again when my mother was pushing me up to a sitting position.

"Come on, Dora, I'm taking you home."

I was finally able to talk, and although it came out in a whisper, my mother heard me.

"Mama, please help me."

"Don't worry, Baby, you're safe now. Mama's here. Now, come on, can you get up?"

Jim came over to the couch and put his hands on my arm, as though he was going to help me get up. I was helpless to pull away, but I swear, my mother's voice came out in as close to what I would describe as a growl from a human's mouth.

"Get your hands off her. Don't you think you've done enough already? I am not a hundred percent sure what is going on here, but I plan on getting to the bottom of it. And soon. Now, let's go, Dora, lean on me and we'll stand up together. You can move, it just feels like you can't."

She was right, with a little help from her, and a lot of willpower from me, because I just wanted to get out of there so bad, I stood up and we walked slowly toward the door.

When we got there and she stopped to open she looked back over her shoulder and said, "Don't call me, James, I'll call you. When I find out what's going on here I'll let you know what I'm going to do."

As the door closed behind us I heard my father say, "Shit," and I was never so relieved in my whole life.

The decision had been made for me at this point. I was not going to be "telling" on my father and my brothers, my mother was going to be asking me.

Although it may not have seemed as though there was an important difference there, there definitely was. As the youngest child in the family, it was a very negative but unfortunate place to often find oneself playing the role of "tattletale". The choice to tell or not had been taken out of hands.

My mother helped me get into the car. Then she put on my seatbelt and closed my door. The next thing I remembered was pulling into our driveway and then Mom coming around to my side of the car to help me get back out again.

I felt a little bit more alert than I had at Dad's house and told my mother that I was alright and could walk by myself when she tried to hold my arm and lead me to the house.

Fortunately, she didn't entirely believe me, because although she did not hold my arm at first, when I started to fall over into the bushes, she was there to grab me and help me the rest of the way.

We went into the house, Mom helped me change into a nightgown and get into bed. Then she told me to rest for a minute and went to the kitchen to make me some soup.

When she came back she sat at the head of the bed and helped me to sit up so I could lean against her. She wrapped her arms around me and held the bowl so I could eat from it. After I finished the soup she took the bowl from me and put it on my nightstand. Then she leaned against the wall and pulled me back to lay against her.

I closed my eyes and relaxed as she rubbed my legs and spoke softly to me. I wasn't even sure what she said, but being in my own bed, with the heat from the soup spreading through my body and the warmth of her voice soothing my thoughts, I felt safer than I had in months. I closed my eyes and felt myself beginning to drift off the sleep, but then I felt something strange.

She moved her hand down my leg and toward my foot. Then, she took my foot gently, but firmly in her hand and separated my big toe from the rest. I lolled my head to the side and opened my eyes, to see what was going on. She reached behind her back and grabbed a needle.

Using her mouth to remove the cover, she forced a small bit of liquid into the air and then buried the needle in between my toes, pressing the plunger and forcing the liquid into me. It wasn't nighttime, so I had no idea why she was giving me medicine.

She realized I was watching her and there was no way she couldn't not feel my body tense up against hers. The confirmation of my father's involvement in my brother's death made me a little bit suspicious - even of my mother. Stacy's suspicion about her injecting me between my toes came back in spades and I wondered why I was ever so stupid to trust her.

"You rest now and we'll talk later."

She never gave me the shot and left me before, always sitting with me and talking until I went to sleep, so my suspicion turned to confusion and right back to suspicion again.

"I've adjusted your dosage a little bit and you might have nightmares. You did sometimes when you were a little girl and I had to up the dose to match your growth. So just let me know, okay? We need to find the optimum dose."

I nodded and my mother left my room, closing the door behind her. I moved around to get into my usual sleeping position: laying on my side with one of my pillows under my head, and hugging my body pillow up against me.

I listened to the quiet sounds outside. I could hear someone far away moving their lawn. I heard birds singing and the wind gently rustling the leaves on the tree outside my window.

The medicine was kicking in and I started feeling very content. For a minute there, I had been worried about what my mother had been doing and I was afraid she was trying to do the same thing my father was trying to do.

As I snuggled with my pillow, I closed my eyes and heard the crow of a rooster, who was obviously confused about what time of day it was and my eyes flew open as another memory came crashing down.

1977

I am on my way to the beach to collect shells. I don't know where my brothers are. Only Tommy. He is in the graveyard with my grandparents. For the whole year after he died, my brothers were always with me, bringing me to the park or the basketball courts, riding bikes, rollerblading, whatever. They always seemed to want to keep me moving.

I didn't understand it, but I certainly didn't mind it. One day, they just stopped, though, and I found myself the way I was before, just hanging around and not doing much. The only difference is now I don't have Tommy to hang around with, because he never minded spending time with me.

I don't know a lot of our neighbors. The houses on my road are pretty far apart and there aren't many kids in our neighborhood, just a lot of old people. I walk around the corner and look over to my right because I hear a loud squawking noise and then a thud.

Nothing, and I mean nothing could prepare me for what I see: Jim, covered in blood, is holding a headless chicken in one hand and an ax in the other.

I have no idea whose house he is at and what he is doing, but I freeze. Jim drops the chicken onto a pile of other headless chickens and scurries to grab another one. He holds it against the tree and then swings the ax, chopping the head from the body. He lets the chicken go and it runs away and starts to run in circles.

My mother always says, "I've been running around like a chicken with its head cut off" and I had no idea what that meant; until then.

I can't be sure, because the wind picked up and made a sort of howling sound, but I thought I heard Jim laugh. That was enough to break me from my trance, and I turned to run.

I hadn't realized it, but Patrick and Donald had snuck up behind me. Patrick grabbed me and held tight against his body, grasping my chin with his hand so I couldn't turn my head away and covering my mouth with his other hand so I couldn't scream.

Donald put his fingers around my eyes, one above and one below, and pulled so I couldn't shut my eyes. We stayed that way for three or four more rounds - Jimmy chased and caught a chicken.

He held it against the tree. He swung the ax and chopped off its head. He let it and go and watched it run in circles until it dropped, dead. He laughed. He picked up the dead chicken and tossed it onto the pile of other headless chickens. He chased and caught a chicken…

Patrick let me go and I dropped to my knees.

My two brothers ran away, laughing, and I looked up at my oldest murdering brother, who had on a Walkman and his back to me, so he was unaware that I was flopped in the road, crying.

Chapter 29

1982

I woke up when my mother came in with a plateful of food for me.

"Good morning, Sunshine!"

I must have looked confused because she said, "That's right, you slept from four o'clock right through the whole night. I made breakfast. I wasn't sure if you'd want to eat in here, or if you want to come to the kitchen."

"I'll come out. Is the door locked?"

"I'm not sure. Why? You have nothing to worry about. Nobody is coming here, okay?"

I noticed my mother looked very different than she usually did. She always wore pantsuits, or skirts and blouses. Even if she was just hanging around at home she dressed kind of formally.

Now she was wearing a flowing white dress that looked like something hippies might have worn in the sixties. Her hair was usually in a tight bun, but this morning it was braided loosely and rested on one of her shoulders.

Weird, I had never seen her look like that before, but also I never had to hang around with her on the day when she was going to find out her husband and her sons killed her other son.

We went to the kitchen, and after I made her check to make sure the doors were locked, I sat down and ate.

We talked about things like school and basketball while I ate, neither said anything about what we were both dying to discuss: she because she obviously had some information, but needed to know the rest, and me because the information was burning up inside me and I was finally going to get it out.

When I finished eating, we went into the living room.

After I was settled on the couch, Mom came over and gave me another shot, in between two different toes this time. I wondered again why she didn't give me a shot normally, like in my arm, but I felt the energy drain from my body and couldn't ask.

She inquired if I had any nightmares or any other side effects. When I told her no she said that was good. She sat down sideways in a chair, with her legs hanging over the arm, the way she told us to never, ever sit.

Between the way she looked and the way she was acting, I was kind of freaking out. Something seemed way off, yet she was my mother, and it was time for me to talk.

"I want you to start from the beginning. Tell me what you saw, what you heard, what you remember. Please don't leave anything out, not to spare my feelings, or because you aren't sure of something. I need to know everything. If there is anything you are unsure of, I can help you fill in the blanks and we'll figure it out together, okay?"

The medicine was really starting to kick in at that point and it was hard for me to hold myself up.

I lay down and started my story from the sleepover I had with Stacy, Laurie, and Brandy, leaving out the 'shrooms situation, of course, and talked until I got to the part where I was at Dad's house and he and Jim were talking about have to "take care of it either way" while I was on the couch there, unable to move.

I didn't look at my mother the whole time I was talking, because like she said, I might find myself leaving details out if I noticed by the look on her face that I was upsetting her.

When I finished, though, I looked up at her. I expected to be focused on the look on her face, but instead I was weirded out, because she was wearing her regular clothes, a dark blue pants suit, with her hair done in a tight bun.

I hadn't noticed her leave to get changed, but obviously she had. Maybe I had dozed for a little while. Even though the medicine was nothing like what dad had given me, I usually went right to sleep after I took it and it definitely made me tired.

"So, let me get this straight," she said. "You actually have the piece of the antenna in your bedroom closet? Right here, right now?"

"Yes."

"I'm going to grab it. Don't move."

She left the room and came back a minute later, empty-handed, but wearing the white dress again, with her hair in the messy braid.

"Mom, I think I need to go take a nap. I feel kind of weird."

"That's fine. I'll wake you up at lunchtime."

It was kind of funny that she wanted me to tell her about my dreams because it might be a side effect of the medicine, but when I told her I felt weird, she didn't even ask about it.

I probably would have told her that I couldn't tell if I was dreaming or awake. I went back to my bedroom and got into bed.

When I closed my eyes, it felt like I was spinning around, but it wasn't long before I was asleep, and dreaming again.

I'm in the middle of my village holding Chip and not even realizing that three dogs are chasing him. I spin around, wearing my own white eyelet hippie dress and I laugh as the bottom fans out and spins with me.

Money falls all around me and I laugh and laugh as it gets caught in my hair, my mouth, my clothes.

I stop spinning when I realize the huskies with my brother's faces are watching me, growling. I hold Chip tight and take a step back. I bump into someone. I look over my shoulder and my mother is there.

Her white dress matches mine, and her braid pushes against me as she leans close and whispers in my ear, "Shh, don't move."

Then she steps next to me, points at the husky that has Jim's face and says, "Bad dog!"

Jim/husky whimpers and lays on the ground at my mother's feet.

The other dogs, the ones with Patrick's and Donny's faces back away until I can no longer see them.

"Dora, open your eyes. Look at the dog, Dora, look at his face."

I squeeze Chip tighter and look down at the husky and notice that his face is a regular dog's face.

"Not now, Dora. Always."

Had I said something out loud? I don't remember saying anything. Chip begins to wiggle in my arms. He barks and wags his tail.

I can no longer hold him and he jumps to the ground. The husky and Chip go around and around in a circle, trying to smell each other's butts.

They go faster and faster, so fast that I can't see them anymore, they are just a blur.

The blur slows and comes into focus, but Chip is no longer chasing the husky's tail, he is laying limp in its mouth, blood dripping from him and splattering onto my mother's bare feet.

The husky drops Chip in front of my mother, like he is giving her a gift. My mother removes a sweater she has tied around her shoulders that I didn't notice before she was wearing.

She puts it over Chip, who is no longer Chip, but a mangled, bloody, and unrecognizable blob, and she says, "This is what has always happened."

Although it is good that she covered him because I don't want to see him, I shiver as her white sweater turns red as soon as she puts it down.

Chapter 30

1983

I rolled over and opened my eyes and was very confused. I was pretty sure that the last time I went to sleep, I was in my bed, but now I was on the couch. The days and nights seemed to be meshing together. I couldn't tell if I had been there for only one day or if it had been several.

I only remembered eating dinner once and breakfast one time, too, but there seemed to be too many memories packed into that one day - too many discussions that my mother and I had - me telling her what I remembered seeing and she explaining why I thought I had seen that and what I had really seen. Or had those been dreams?

I pushed the blankets off with my legs and sat up, then I froze, my father and Jim were in the room with me. I hoped I was dreaming. When I blinked and they were still there, I knew it was not a dream.

"Mom!" I shouted.

"It's okay, Dora. I asked them to come."

She came to the couch and stood near me. She took my hand in hers and turned so she was facing my father and my brother.

"Dora has told me some pretty interesting things."

"What?" My father sat up straight in his chair. "What did she tell you?"

"It seems as though there's been some things going on around here that I didn't know anything about."

"Like what?"

Now it was Jim's turn to sit at attention.

"I think you should listen to our side of the story before you believe anything she says. You know she's always been a storyteller, that's even what you used to call her."

It was going exactly like I thought it would. Jim was setting things up to make it out like I made everything up, for what reason, well, he'd find one. I just had to hope my mother didn't believe him. She had seemed to believe what I told her, but I knew Jim could be convincing.

"She told me that she remembers it - all of it. I don't know how the two of you managed to mess this up. She even has the antenna. She went during the Open House and it was still there. It never occurred to you two geniuses to get rid of it?"

She walked over to the love seat where my father was sitting and sitting next to him, picked up a cup that was on the coffee table.

I wasn't sure that I heard her right. It sounded like my mother had just said something about them getting rid of the antenna.

"Mama?"

"Oh my God, Dora, you need to shut up already."

My mother took a sip of her coffee. I think, probably for the first time in my entire life, I was speechless.

She turned and faced my father, "She hasn't shut her mouth for two days. I'm going fucking insane over here listening to her."

"Is everything set? You said you were going to be able to take care of it, so we're okay?" my father asked.

"Not exactly. Let's just say, I've worked out a solution. It's not the ideal, not what I hoped for, but it'll be fine."

"I'm not sure I like the sound of that."

Jim put his feet up on the coffee table and all my mother had to do was look at him, and he took his feet down and sat up.

"What is it then? Not something with that fucked up medicine?"

"Watch your mouth!" my mother scolded, taking a sip of tea.

"I can't say it, but you can? Besides it is fucked up, it's not like there is another word to describe it."

"Speaking of the medicine."

My mother got up, handed her cup to my father and came over to me. She opened the drawer of the end table, took a needle and jabbed it between my toes. This time she didn't bother rubbing it after, she just went back and sat down with Dad, taking her coffee back and drinking some more.

"Okay, so I'll try to explain this so you'll understand. Back when you boys - when what happened - we used the medicine to do what Dr Craven calls Memory Replacement Therapy. It was for war veterans, when they came back and were traumatized by what they saw. They could give them an injection, talk to them and suggest that they saw something different than what they actually saw."

I dropped back onto the pillow. The medicine was working faster now, and I had to fight to keep the conversation straight.

"Like what?" Jim asked.

"For instance, they didn't actually see their best friend step on a land mine and get blown to bits, they were at their campsite all day, smoking pot and watching their friends do stand-up comedy or imitations of famous actors, something like that."

"Did it work?" Jim asked.

"Not so well, most of the time the memories would come back within a month or so. They found if they suggested the alternate memory and then had them participate in rigorous recreational activities, like football or basketball, it worked better. It didn't give them time to think about the real memory, until the suggested memory was, how do I put this, solidified? At least that's what they thought at first, but then they determined it was endocannabinoids, a hormone that is released during exercise."

"That's what we did with Dora, then, right?"

"Exactly. Every night I brought her through guided imagery, in other words I explained in detail what I wanted her to think she saw, and then during the day you guys kept her busy, so she never had time to think. It worked pretty well. Children are obviously better candidates for this type of therapy. It seems she heard a song that was playing that night recently and that's what triggered the memory. I'm not sure why the medicine stopped working. She's grown quite a bit, maybe I didn't up the dose enough. I'm pretty much overdosing her right now, until we get this sorted out."

"What does she remember then?" Dad picked up the other cup and took a sip.

"Unfortunately, she remembers what she actually saw, not what I convinced her she saw."

"What did you convince her she saw?" Jim asked

"I sort of suggested that she might have actually seen Tommy shoot himself."

"Mom!"

"I know. I know. It was pretty harsh, but I didn't have a choice. Look how well it turned out, for what, six years now? She forgot what she actually saw and she suppressed the memory that was supplanted. We really couldn't have asked for a better scenario."

"Except for it to have continued," my father said.

"Well, of course," my mother agreed. "But you have to admit, she had it pretty good for the last few years. I didn't plan for any of this to happen, you know that, James."

She looked at him and he nodded.

She turned to Jim, "Tommy gave me no choice, really, and now Dora's not giving me a choice either. What was I supposed to do? Just sit here while your father's good name got destroyed? Don't fool yourself, Jim, you're not the first person in this family with aspirations. Your father's list of political goals was every bit as long as yours, if not longer. And Tommy, whether he was found guilty or not, didn't really matter, a trial would have destroyed us. All of us. No matter what the outcome was, we would have been all done. A suicide? At least that would gain us some sympathy, make people forget about Tommy and the girl.

"Today, when someone mentions Tommy's name, that's what people remember. The suicide. Not the rape. God knows I didn't necessarily want that stigma, but what are you going to do? I tried to give that girl's father every opportunity to kill Tommy himself, but he wouldn't. Goddamn pacifists. So, I did what I had to do then, and I'll do what I have to do now."

"What do you need me to do right now?" my father asks.

"It might be a good idea to feed her. I haven't given her anything at all since she's been here."

"Anybody else?" my father got up and headed to the kitchen.

"We should probably all have something. We're going to be busy for the next day or so. Might not get a chance to eat."

I was totally confused because I remembered eating, but my fear trumped my confusion. What did she mean by we're going to be busy? Setting up my suicide?

I had been so afraid of my brother and father, sure my mother was my savior and now I knew she was in on it. I felt my lower lip start to quiver. I shut my eyes and pressed my lips together. I thought it would be better for me if they thought I was asleep.

I guess I did fall asleep, because when I opened my eyes again, I was in my room and I was alone. At least I thought I was, but I wasn't sure.

The reason I had opened my eyes in the first place is because I felt hot breath on my ear and heard a voice, but nobody was there when I looked.

The voice had said, "Dora, everyone is asleep. You can escape. They are going to kill you. Leave now."

I sat up and looked around to be sure. The room was definitely empty. I knew I must have been dreaming.

Nobody had spoken to me, but at the same time, the voice had been right. Neither my parents nor my brother was in the room with me and the house was totally silent. They were all definitely sleeping.

As for them killing me, that was something I was already afraid of and even if it was just my subconscious that spoke to me, it was right and the time to escape was right now.

I slipped out of bed and without turning on my lights, I found my clothes and shoes and quietly got dressed. I quietly eased my door open, just enough so I could squeeze through and then I closed it quietly behind me. I stood there for a minute and listened.

Silence.

I tiptoed to the front door and eased it open - just enough to squeeze through. It squeaked anyway. I winced, but nothing stirred. No footsteps. No voices. No door creaks. I pulled it closed behind me, careful not to let the latch click too loud.

The air outside was damp and cool, smelling like pine and ocean and something else - something metallic. My bare feet stung against the front steps, but I didn't care. I ran. Down the walkway. Past the stone marker. Through the side yard.

My heart was pounding so loud it drowned out everything else, like it was the only thing in the world that could make sound. I reached the edge of the road and hesitated - just for a moment.

That's all it was. A flicker of doubt. What if I was wrong? What if I was just crazy, like they said? What if they were really just trying to help me?

Behind me, I heard the door slam. Footsteps. Running. "Dora!"

My mother's voice. She sounded scared.

I turned and saw them coming - her and my brother, both of them, barefoot and running toward me, hair wild, faces panicked.

My foot slipped forward into the road. Lights. A car. Headlights barreling around the bend. No time to think. Then I felt it - her hands on my shoulders. Grabbing me, pulling me back. Saving me. And it that instant I was flooded with shame. My mother loved me. She would never hurt, try to kill me.

But then - I felt it. The pressure shifted. She wasn't pulling. She was pushing. Hard. I stumbled forward, right into the path of the oncoming car.

Tires screeched. Horn blared. I froze. The car swerved - barely missed me. I felt the wind of it scrape past. Then silence again.

I was on the ground. My knees scraped. My elbow bleeding. And my mother, standing above me, her chest heaving, eyes wide with something that was not relief. Guilt? Rage? I didn't know. But in that moment, every doubt I had was gone.

She hadn't tried to save me.

She'd tried to finish what they started.

1977

I sink down to the floor. I cover my face with my hands. I don't want to see my brother on the roof. I start to cry now.

My Mommy and Daddy come running up the stairs. Mommy grabs me up and hugs me, rubbing my hair.

Daddy climbs out the window and crawls across the roof to Tommy and shakes his shoulder like he is trying to wake him up.

"Tommy! Tommy!"

Then he turns and says to my mother, "Rainy! Get her out of here!"

My brothers - the ones who are alive - scramble in the window and run past me. Jimmy still has the antenna in his hands and I see by the dull flicker light of the bare attic bulb that there is something red on the end. Wet. Shiny

They are all yelling to each other to hurry and get away. Jimmy is yelling about cleaning the antenna and "The Parent Pact" and directing Pat to get a gun so they can make it look like Tommy did it to himself.

My Mommy rushes down the stairs, still carrying me, telling me that everything is going to be okay, and that she loves me.

I tell her that I love her, too, and I do. I feel like my heart is going to burst with how much I love my Mommy.

Chapter 31

1983

When I wake up in the morning, the sunshine is coming through my window and warming the side of my face. I yawn and stretch and it feels so good. I pull my blankets up to my chin and just snuggle for a minute, feeling warm and safe and comfortable in my crisp clean sheets.

I could stay in bed all day, I feel so comfy, but I would get in trouble. I get up and use the bathroom and then I get dressed and go to the dining room for breakfast.

Nobody else is in there, and I'm glad. I have bacon and eggs and an English muffin on the side. Everything tastes so good, even the orange juice I drink to wash it all down. When I am done eating, I clean up my dishes and go into the television room. I watch a game show that is playing until he calls me.

I go into his office and sit in my favorite chair.

He smiles at me, "Good morning, Dora. How are you today?"

"I'm great."

I sit sideways in the chair, my legs hanging over the arm and swinging back and forth. I know he won't yell at me like my mother does. I'm right, he doesn't.

"That's really great to hear. You didn't feel so good yesterday."

"I feel much better. Can we go to the beach today?"

"No, Dora. I'm afraid not. It's too far away, remember? I told you that before."

I try hard to remember if he did tell me, but I can't. It doesn't really make much sense because we're surrounded by water. How could the beach be too far away? He makes no sense at all.

"Dora, you are no longer on the Island. We're in Taunton. The closest beach is over an hour away. Now, do you want to talk about your family today?"

"What about them?"

"Would you like to see them? Your mother? Maybe your father or your brother Jim?"

"I don't think I can."

"Why not?" He takes out a notebook and writes something down.

"I think they're in jail. I'm not sure if I can go see them there."

"They're in jail? Why is that?"

I can't believe he doesn't know.

"They killed my brother Tommy. It seems to me like you should already know this. If you know me, then you must know that."

"They killed your brother? That is not what you told me yesterday."

I try to remember instead of asking him, but I have no memory of yesterday at all, "What did I tell you yesterday?"

"You told me that Tommy killed himself and that you saw it. You were standing in the attic and you watched him."

I couldn't help, I burst out laughing, "That's right! That's what she wants you to believe!"

"Who is she?' He was writing again, faster now.

"Not just her. All of them."

"All of them?"

"Yes, my mother, my brothers…"

"They want me to think you witnessed your brother killing himself?"

"Right. They all want you to believe that."

"The day before that you told me that your brother was in the Witness Protection Program and he was living in another state with a new identity. Do you remember that?"

"Okay. You are just totally trying to confuse me now. I bet she has you doing that, huh?"

"Who is she, Dora?"

"Never mind. I just want to go home. When can I go?"

"We need to make sure that you're safe before we can send you home."

"I'm safe! What does that even mean?"

"You do erratic things. You run away from your mother. You almost got hit by a car running away from her. Do you remember that?"

"She pushed me in front of that car! I wasn't running away from her at all. That's just what she said when the car swerved out of the way and didn't hit me."

"And, again, that is not what you told me yesterday. You said nothing like that ever happened, you never almost got hit by a car."

"Can I go now? Like usual this conversation is going absolutely nowhere."

"Sure. I just need to roll up your sleeve so I can give you your medicine before you go."

He opened his desk drawer and took out a needle. I rolled up my sleeve.

"I don't understand why the nurses give me other medicine but you give me this."

"I've told you before, they're not trained to administer this medicine."

He came out from behind the desk, holding the needle up in the air.

"That makes no sense. They're nurses aren't they?"

"Only a doctor is able to give an intravenous medication here."

"What does that even mean? Intravenous?"

"A shot,' he plunges the needle into my arm. "You can go now. We'll talk again tomorrow?"

"Like it'll do any good. You'll just tell me a bunch of lies. Her lies. Then you'll give me that fucked up medicine again. It's pretty predictable," I say over my shoulder as I walk out.

"Okay, Dora, have a nice day."

"Thanks. You, too."

I slam the door behind me.

Clinical Summary:

Patient Adorable "Dora" Culligan

Patient AC is a fourteen year, 10 month-old Caucasian female student who was admitted to the acute psychiatric ward with a three day history of confusion and disturbed behavior. She was restless, disorientated, paranoid, and had not been eating or sleeping. She was admitted following an acute episode of paranoia, when she ran from her mother and into the road, almost being struck by a vehicle. Prior to the admission she was extensively investigated on a medical ward to rule out an organic cause for her presentation. All the investigations proved normal. On the ward, she presents as emotionally labile and agitated. Her behavior is chaotic: at times she paces up and down the halls or lays down on the floor. On a few occasions, she has assaulted staff when they tried to prevent her from leaving the ward. She is often disorientated and has poor concentration. She alternates between believing that she saw her brothers murder another brother, or that she witnessed this brother committing suicide, and believing that this brother is the recipient of an alternate identity through the Federal Witness Protection Program. She was diagnosed at eight years-old with a mood disorder and childhood onset schizophrenia. Her diagnosis has been updated to include a formal thought disorder. AC has described second person auditory hallucinations. She continues to alternate between her contradicting beliefs regarding her brother and her family. She is currently prescribed 50mg s of oral Thorazine administered 3 times daily. It is advised that she remain hospitalized until therapeutic levels of Thorazine are determined and she presents with coherent and logical thought processes.

Personal notes - REDACTED - It is this professional's opinion that the family keeping the truth from Dora is causing distress. They can give her all the medication in the world (I also don't agree with the use of a medication that is not approved by the FDA) and tell her all the stories they want, but deep down, she knows what happened and it is causing these false memories. I understand why the family continues with this ruse, I just don't agree with it.

Epilogue

1984

When Dora woke up in the morning, the first thing she saw was the curtain on her canopy bed frame. It was almost exactly the same as the one she had when she was a little kid, a bed that looked like it belonged in a princesses' quarters. In fact, her whole room was pretty much the same as it had been in the old house, and she loved it.

When she was away at the hospital, her father had finished the room, and it was just perfect. The second thing she saw was her mother, sitting on the edge of her bed, rubbing her hair, and smoothing it back from her face.

"Good morning, Sunshine," her mother said in the sweet sing-song voice she always used when she said that.

"Good morning, Momma. What time is it?"

"It's time for you to get up. It's almost ten o'clock. I have your breakfast warming in the oven, but if we leave it much longer, it will be dried out. You're also past due for your medicine. Let's go. Get up," her mother said, reaching for her blankets.

Dora sat up and slipped her foot out from under the covers.

"I thought Dr. Craven was going to work on it so I don't have to get shots anymore, make it into a capsule or something."

"He's working on it, honey. These things take time."

Her mother held the needle straight up in the air and pushed on the plunger so a little bit of liquid spurted out, then she gently inserted the needle between Dora's toes and pushed the plunger again, this time all the way.

She removed the needle, and gently rubbed her fingertips over the injection spot. Then she kissed Dora's check, and helped her put on her slippers.

"Probably by the time he gets it done, I won't even have to take it anymore."

"I'm pretty sure you'll have to keep taking it, so that won't be an issue."

"For how long?"

"Well, maybe forever.

"Forever?" Dora asked incredulously.

"In pill form it won't matter, right? I understand you not wanting to get shots forever."

"I guess," Dora replied.

"Get dressed. I'll see you in the kitchen."

Dora put on a new pair of jeans that her mother had bought for her at the mall on the way home from the hospital. They were the new fad in jeans, embroidered flowers on the right leg from the hip to the knee, and on the left leg from the knee to the ankle. Dora hadn't seen them before until her mother got them for her. She had been a little out of touch since she had been in Taunton for six months, but she was home now and was catching up.

Two nights ago, Jim, Pat, and Donny had come over for dinner. Even though the new house didn't have a dining room, their father had kept the table and put it in the kitchen of the new house. It was a little too fancy for the room, but Dora thought it looked okay, and she liked the fact that it was the same table that she ate at her whole life. There were a lot of good memories from sitting around that table.

When her brothers had arrived, Jim by himself, and Pat and Donny together, they had all given Dora big hugs and everyone had gravitated to the same seats where they had sat when they were kids. Their father sat at one end, and their mother sat opposite of him. Jim and Pat sat on one side of the table and Donny and Dora sat on the other.

They had talked about when they were kids and laughed about all the crazy things they had done. The only time the conversation had gotten serious was when somebody mentioned Chip.

Dora's face had clouded over and she lamented about how much she hated huskies. It was a night of laughter, and memories, but later it became all about confessions. It started with Donny telling his mother how he took money from her pocketbook all the time.

"But I didn't grow up to be a thief, so I guess it worked out alright, besides whenever I got money, I would always put it back."

Their mother had laughed and told Donny she always knew about it, and she knew he put it back, which was the only reason why she never said anything. Dora's brothers admitted to their father that they used to play soccer in their fort. Their father always said soccer was a sport that only "wussies" played, so they never wanted to admit that they liked it.

"Why do you think we didn't build a tree fort like normal kids?" Jim had asked.

The confession session turned a little more serious when the kids told their parents about Piggily-Wiggily. Now that Dora was older, she realized it wasn't as serious of a situation that she had thought it was when she was eight.

It had been an accident, and their mother and father hadn't been mad at all. In fact, their father had sheepishly admitted he was glad when Piggily-Wiggily was gone.

"The damn thing smelled like a Christmas tree with ornaments made out of shit."

Everyone had laughed when he said that, and Dora felt the tension she had been feeling drain from her body.

With that confession out of the way, Dora felt she might as well go ahead and blurt out that she hid in the attic and spied on her brothers.

"Yeah, we know, Dora. We always knew when you were there. No matter what you plan on being when you grow up, don't make it a spy. You're not very good," Jim had said. "Everything we said was planned out to mess with you."

Dora hadn't been terribly surprised by that. She had been surprised when she was a kid that they had never caught her. The boys went on to tell their parents about other times they had "messed" with Dora: when they had locked in the shed at the graveyard and held her over the water after going to see Jaws. They had all told her that they were sorry about doing those things.

"Brothers. Doing rotten things to their little sisters since the dawn of time. I could tell you some stories about brothers and their sisters that make those things look like playing Tiddlywinks," their mother had said.

"What about the chicken thing?" Dora had asked.

"That was just a shit show. An accident. You were never, ever supposed to see that."

"Why were you even doing that?" Dora had asked.

"Mr. Thompson hired me to kill them. He raised chicken to sell for the meat and he was getting on in years, couldn't really do it himself anymore. It's not like I was doing it for fun or something. Is that what you thought?"

"Well…" Dora began.

"I wasn't," Jim said. "You were snooping around, spying on me, as usual, and you happened to come by at the wrong time. I tried to talk to you about it, but you wouldn't listen to me. You just ran away from me like I was a murderer or something. I felt wicked bad, but then you seemed to forget about it, and I did, too. The next year when Mr. Thompson tried to hire me again, I said I couldn't do it, and I really couldn't. It made me sick, actually, and the fact that you saw it, well that was just horrible."

"But you laughed when you did it, when they ran around."

"Laughed? No, Dora, I was retching. I actually did end up puking."

Dora let what Jim said sink in for a while and said nothing. Although she thought that she remembered it differently, what she did remember seemed so hazy and distant, that Jim's explanation seemed entirely plausible.

"If that's it for the Culligan family's version of True Confessions, I have something I need to talk to you about. Let's finish eating, and then I want to go downstairs to talk."

After dinner everyone had gone into the basement. There was no recreation room set up in this new house, but her father had stored a lot of stuff from the old house down there. There were boxes stacked up everywhere and the old pool table was set up in the corner piled high with old books and magazines. The couch that had been in the old basement was there, it too was being used as a place to stack stuff.

The boys got to work right away, moving boxes off the couch and stacking them against the wall. When it was all cleared off, they sat. Dora sat on the arm of the couch until her mother gave her the evil eye, then she slipped down onto the cushions between Jim and Donny.

At first, she thought there was something about that couch, some reason that she didn't ever want to sit on it, but she couldn't quite grasp what it was, so she just sat. Their father had perched on the edge of the pool table and their mother sat in a reclining chair that had been in their television room at the old house.

Their father had sighed heavily before he began to speak. "I know it seems rather odd that I asked you all down here to talk, but it seemed like the safest place."

"What's up, Dad?" Jim asked.

"I also know that it's never been anything that we've talked about, but it seems important now, with what's happened with Dora."

"Seriously, Dad," Pat said. "What are we talking about already?"

"Tommy, your brother Tommy. I need to make sure that you all understand what happened. It became obvious to us that the situation was volatile. We, your mother and I, aren't certain what you know, what you believe, but we now know that it caused Dora some great distress in her life and we want to make sure you are all okay."

"About what? What happened to Tommy? The truth? Or what is supposed to be the truth?"

"He's dead," Donny said. "He killed himself."

"Is that what you truly believe?" their mother had asked.

Donny gulped and shook his head. He looked away from his parents.

"I know we told you that we were never going to talk about it again, but this is the one exception. You're right, Donny, that was the official story, the story that we told everyone, but you all know the true story, right?"

"Is this a trick?" Pat asked. "To see what we say?"

"Honestly, it's not. Jim, you're not afraid to say it, right?"

Dora couldn't take it anymore and she blurted out, "He is in the Witness Protection Program, right?"

Her brothers and her parents all stayed very still. Nobody said anything.

"Yes, Dora, that is correct," her mother finally said.

"Do you remember why? Jim?"

"He didn't actually rape that girl. He was doing something…well bad, with his friend, the girl's brother. But after that her brother got an idea and had boys pay him to sleep with his sister. Tommy testified about it, so they got him outta' here and made it look like he was dead."

"Where is he? Can we see him?" Donny asked.

"We don't even know where he lives, but we get periodic correspondence from the Witness Protection agents. He is doing just fine in his new life."

"That's right. So now everyone is aware of the actual situation and, just like when you were younger, this is it. Nobody is to talk about it again, okay?" their father said.

"Hold on, Dad," Jim said. "I guess I don't really understand all this, never did. Why did they fake his death like that?"

"The Witness Protection Program was trying a new thing back then, faking deaths. That way nobody would look for the person. It worked when the program was new but because everyone knew about what they were doing, relocating people, people got found. In fact, there are a lot of people who think our Island has been used many times as a place for people to relocate."

"I'm pretty sure Mr. James, the butcher in Vineyard Haven is in it. He never answers when you call his name. It usually takes two or three times to get his attention, like it's not really even his name."

"Maybe he just has a bit of hearing loss," their father had offered.

"Maybe," their mother had said, laughing. "But at the same time, he kind of looks like a gangster."

"You've been watching too many movies," their father had said.

"That could be true, too, but think about it, what better job for an old gangster than a butcher?"

"Ma! That's terrible," Jim said.

"I'm just joking," their mother amended, but she wasn't smiling or laughing, and then she sat back in the chair and didn't say anything else.

"So, then what about Tommy? Where is he? What is he doing?" Jim asked.

"Well, we can't tell you where he is; we don't even have that information, but recently we found out that he graduated from college with a degree in mechanical engineering. He is also recently married, and they are expecting a baby in the early summer," their father said.

As she spoke, Dora had that funny unexplainable feeling of déjà vu, as though she had heard all this before, but not from her father or in the basement, and not with her brothers hearing it, too.

She felt like she could almost remember when she did hear it, and also that she knew exactly what her father was going to say before he said it, but it wasn't quite...

"Can we see him? Can we talk to him?" Jim asked excitedly, interrupting Dora's train of thought.

Their parents looked at each other, as though they wanted the other one to answer the question. Their mother broke the gaze first, and looked across the basement, so their father answered.

"That won't be possible. It is a very secure program that he is in. Any contact with people from his former life could jeopardize his safety. You understand, right? We wouldn't want to do anything that could cause him any problems, now would we?"

"Of course not," said Donny. Everyone else nodded in agreement.

"I suppose we could ask the agents, and maybe you could write him letters. They could deliver them, and as long as there was nothing that identified who or where we are, I think the agents will agree. I can't think of any reason they would give to say no. Whether or not they would let him write back, I'm not so sure about that," their mother said.

"Will we ever be able to see him?" Pat asked. "Maybe in like a few years, like when the people he testified about die off or something?"

"I don't think that's how it works," their father answered. "But I will ask. It doesn't hurt to ask, right?"

"Is that it, then? Any more questions?" their mother asked.

All the kids looked around at each other, then back at their parents and they all shook their heads.

"Okay, so I'll repeat it one more time to make sure you all understand. You do not, under any circumstances, discuss this again. Not among yourselves, and definitely not with anybody else, understand? This could be a matter of life and death for your brother and we've worked too hard and for too long to let anything silly, like 'I have a secret and I just have to tell you' kind of thing. It could get him killed. This is not a game. Do you all understand?" their father asked.

Again, everyone nodded.

"Okay, that settles it then. If anyone has questions that are really troubling you, you can ask your mother or me. We don't need anything like what happened with Dora happening again. We will come down here and talk about it. Does everybody understand this? Let's head upstairs then. Dora, are you ready to go outside? Are you boys taking her out?"

"Sure," Dora jumped up from the couch and bounded up the stairs, two at a time. Her father, Pat, and Donny followed behind, but her mother and Jim didn't get up.

"Dora, go change into your track shorts. You won't be comfortable in jeans at the track practicing for the meet," her mother yelled up to her.

"So, what do you think?" Jim asked when the upstairs door closed. "Is she okay? Is this going to work out this time?"

"Yes, Jim, everything is going to be fine."

"That's what you said before, and it wasn't."

"Well, this time it will be. I've upped her medication dose and her exercise program will be doubled."

"I don't even understand the exercise thing," Jim said.

"Nobody does. It just seems to help with the supplanting. When the group who exercised was compared to the group who just sat around after they got their shots, the active group had better results. Something to do with the medicine and its reaction to endocannabinoids or endorphins."

"Whatever that means. Anyway, do you think we're doing the right thing here?"

"Yes, we are."

"I'm not so sure I agree with that," Jim practically whispered.

"Are you suggesting we tell her the truth? Do you really think that will help? It will absolutely destroy her! She loved Tommy."

"I just feel like this is destroying her," Jim ventured hesitantly.

Rainy gritted her teeth, "Are you serious right now? Dora thinking he killed himself, or even that you killed him, I'll never know how she came up with that one, was the best we could hope for. For some reason this Witness Protection thing never sticks, but I think what we added this time is going to help."

"What did you add?" Jim asked.

"We have you boys on the roof arguing about if he should testify or not."

"I know why she thinks we killed him," Jim said, his voice quieter now. "Pat told her."

Rainy froze, "Pat?"

"Yeah. One night, after you gave her the meds but left the room, he went in and did the whole guided imagery thing like you do. Sat down, real serious, told her he was going to tell her the truth."

Rainy stared at him, "What truth?"

"That I stabbed Tommy. With an old antenna pole from the roof. Said Donny helped hold him down."

Jim gave a bitter laugh, "Told her it was all a lie. That you'd made up the suicide story. He did it just like you did. The guided imagery thing."

"What the hell would make him say that?"

"He was mad at me and Donny for some reason or another and he thought it would be funny. Not to do it, but to tell us that he did. He told her that what you told her was a lie and he was going to tell her the truth," Jim explained. "He was just joking. He didn't really think she would remember it."

"Is that all he told her?"

"Nope. He told her that we killed Chip and that Donny and I molested her."

"Why the hell would he do that? I'm going to bust his ass," Rainy said.

"Like I said, he never in a million years thought she would remember it."

"I'll have to try to figure out how to undo that. I'm perplexed as to why she remembered all that. It must have been why there was so much difficulty making her believe what I told her."

"Anyway, I think everyone did real good acting tonight, like they really wanted to see Tommy."

"Yeah, you're all great actors. That's not the point. It's her retaining it."

"I just feel like if we told her the truth -"

"Do you want to do it, Jim? Tell her the truth?

"No."

"So, you can just go up to her and say, Dora, you want to know what actually happened to Tommy? Because I'll tell you right now…"

"Ma…"

"Come on. We'll go upstairs right now and you tell her."

"No!"

Jim took off up the stairs and slammed the door behind him.

1976

Dora woke up to the racket her brothers were making on the roof, even though she usually slept through it. She rolled over and pulled the pillow over her head, trying to drown out their laughter and the annoying song they were listening to. It was somebody singing about a highway to hell, and Dora didn't know why they liked it, or why they had to listen to it so loud.

She got up and flung her blankets away. She glanced over at her bathrobe and slippers, but didn't put them on, even though she knew her mother would get mad if she saw her without her being covered up.

At that moment she didn't care, because she was so aggravated. As she turned the corner toward the entrance to the attic, she glanced over her shoulder and saw that her parents' door was shut tight, and she breathed a sigh of relief.

She wanted to yell at her brothers for waking her up and didn't want her mother to stop her. When she got to the bottom of the stairs, she changed her mind, though. About her bathrobe and slipper. She wished she had put them on, because it was freezing.

Her brothers left the window open and she could smell their smoke. She wondered why her mother was so dumb she never seemed to smell it, not the cigarette or pot smell. In fact, she actually believed them when they told her that the smell of pot was incense.

The music was coming from Tommy's room - I'm on a highway to hell - and she wanted to go in his room and smash the stereo because she hated that song and was so sick of hearing it. She knew she'd get in big trouble though - more than just getting sent to her room and getting her dictionary taken away - the kind of trouble if she did that and there would be no "Parent Pact" to protect her.

Dora started up the stairs. It always seemed so easy when she wasn't looking at them to think about yelling and standing up for herself, but when she got to the landing halfway up that turned a little corner and she saw them through the window on the roof laughing, goofing around, passing a cigarette, her nerve faltered a little.

She could hear the "Ping! Ping!" of the acorns that her brothers always hit with a metal pole they pulled off the old antenna. After a moment, she took a deep breath and started to go ahead.

She stopped again. Not because of nerves that time, but because there was something leaning against the wall on the landing that should not be there. She knew her mother would be really mad if she saw it, so she picked it up and brought it with her.

Now she was not going to just yell at them to keep quiet, she was going to yell at Jim for having something so dangerous in the house. She knew he went out earlier in the day with his friend and his father to the woods looking for deer but didn't know why he would have brought that thing home.

For the second time that night, Dora regretted not taking the time to put on the robe and slippers, because when she got to the top step, she stubbed her toe on its overhang. She was so focused on the pain, it hurt even more than when Piggily-Wiggily bit her, that she hardly noticed that she was falling. She hit the floor hard, but her brain was unable to make sense of how loud the sound was when she hit, and also why it hurt her shoulder. Forget her toe, her shoulder felt like someone hit her with a hammer.

She heard her brothers scream and she knew that although they would yell at her for bothering them, this was different, and she thought it was because she fell. Her mind quickly put together a scenario where they looked in and saw her and that something really bad happened to her shoulder, because they sounded really scared and someone was yelling about blood.

She glanced at her shoulder but didn't see anything. She noticed that she dropped the gun. It had slid across the floor and it lay there, looking like a snake.

She could hear her mother yelling from her room, asking what was going on. Dora just wanted to close her eyes and not have anyone say anything to her. She wanted to become invisible. She wanted to go to her room, close the door and get back into her bed, like she never even got out of it.

She got up and went to the window to get away from her parents, who she realized weren't going to just close their door but were going to come up the stairs. She decided she'd just climb out, go over the peak of the roof and climb down the trellis like her brothers did when they would sneak out, and she'd run away.

She would live in the woods and sneak to the beach at night to catch fish to eat. But she couldn't move. There was something red all over the roof and although she didn't know what it was, it looked slippery and she was already afraid of falling off, never mind if there was something slick under her feet.

"Oh my God! Tommy!"

"Is he dead?"

"Of course he's dead! Look at all the blood"

"What the fuck just happened?"

"Dora!"

"Dora?"

"Dora shot him!"

"What is she doing with a gun?"

"Where did she get a gun from? Jim, is that your gun?"

"Oh my fucking God, she's right there at the window!"

"Get her the fuck out of here!"

Donny jumped in the window and grabbed Dora, dragging her down the stairs. Now her parents were there, and her father took her from Donny, "I've got her. You can go back to your room, too."

Her mother continued past them and hung out the window, "What happened?"

"I don't know, he was standing there one minute, and then he just…"

"What did you see? You had to have seen something!" her mother screamed.

As Dora and her father rounded the corner to her bedroom, Dora whimpered the answer to her mother's question into her father's shoulder.

"Nothing, I didn't see nothing."

Dora's father put her down in her bed, smoothed back her hair and kissed her forehead.

"Don't worry, Princess, your Mommy will be down soon and she'll take care of everything."

"Where's Tommy? What happened to Tommy?"

"Everything's okay, Princess. Go back to sleep. You're having a bad dream."

Dora fell back asleep and woke up later to a sharp pinch in her arm and whispered voices around her, "I don't like this, not one bit."

"Do you have a better idea? She was there and telling people they weren't there at all never works, you can change it up a little, but the basic premise has to stay the same."

"You don't think letting her believe she witnessed a suicide is going to be traumatic? "

"You don't think it's going to be less traumatic than the truth?"

Then Dora felt like she was floating, and then she was comfy in her Mommy's lap, and they snuggled, her

Mommy alternating between rubbing the pinched spot on her arm and smoothing her hair back on her forehead.

"When you got the top of the stairs, you saw Tommy, oh my God, you saw Tommy and he was holding a gun, and then, he held it to up under his chin and pulled the trigger -"

Dora sobbed and her mother pulled her against her shoulder and hugged her.

But Dora didn't know that.

She wasn't there.

She was standing in front of the attic window, feeling the rush of cold air and smelling the smell of her brother's cigarettes, wishing for the second time that night she put on her bathrobe and slippers -

Author's Note

Trigger is a work of fiction, though its emotional roots run deep into real life. I lost my brother to suicide - a sentence that still catches in my throat. The grief that followed wasn't clean or understandable. It was messy, confusing, and full of silence.

There is a stigma around suicide that often prevents people from speaking honestly about it. That silence can be as harmful as the loss itself. This book is not my brother's story, and it's not mine either. But it is built on a familiar emotional terrain - one where trauma is buried, denial is passed down like an heirloom, and truth becomes something you have to dig up alone.

The characters, events, and settings in Trigger are fictional. Any resemblance to real people or incidents is purely coincidental. But the feelings -the gaslighting, the disorientation, the need to remember what others would rather forget - those are real. Fiction gave me a place to explore them safely.

If you've ever lost someone, questioned your own memory, or held a truth that no one else would believe - you're not alone.

You are seen.

ACKNOWLEDGEMENTS

I am deeply grateful to my friend Laura, who believed in me even when I doubted myself - thank you for being my number one champion and cheerleader.

To my dear friend Holli, thank you for encouraging me and listening through every twist and turn of this story.

And, to my husband, I appreciate your ability to listen to every half-finished plot twist and pretend you knew exactly which story I was rambling on about. Somehow, you always knew when I just needed you to nod.

And to my dog, Bradl, who faithfully kept my feet warm while I wrote - your companionship made even the hardest nights easier.

Finally, to every reader who opens this book - thank you for allowing these words, and this story, to find a home in your heart. May it remind you, as it has me, that truth endures and memory matters.